PAPIER-
MACHE

Miranda Innes

PAPIER-
MACHE

Photography by Clive Streeter

DK

DORLING KINDERSLEY
LONDON · NEW YORK · STUTTGART · MOSCOW

A DORLING KINDERSLEY BOOK

Created and produced by
COLLINS & BROWN LIMITED

First American Edition, 1995
2 4 6 8 10 9 7 5 3 1

Published in the United States by
Dorling Kindersley Publishing, Inc.
95 Madison Avenue
New York, New York 10016

ISBN 0-7894-0335-8

A catalog record is available from the Library of Congress.

Project Editor	Heather Dewhurst
Managing Editor	Sarah Hoggett
Senior Editor	Colin Ziegler
U.S. Editor	Laaren Brown
Art Director	Roger Bristow
Designers	Patrick Knowles
	Marnie Searchwell
	Steven Wooster
DTP Designer	Claire Graham
Photography	Clive Streeter

Reproduced by Daylight, Singapore
Printed and bound in France by Pollina

Contents

Getting Started

Shaping, Molding, and Frameworks

Decorative Ideas and Finishes

Introduction

IF PLAYING AROUND in boats is the quintessence of pleasure for two-legged water rats, squelching around with paper pulp is heaven for anyone whose childhood was too short, who never had long enough in the sandbox, or who is simply halfway dextrous and has a mind to make beautiful, quirky and amusing objects for the price of a daily paper.

Papier-mâché is great for all kinds of reasons. To begin with, there is absolutely nothing so conducive of a gratifying sense of smugness as recycling garbage. Who knows? You may even get to read the newspapers that are forming your work of art! As a pastime, it is impeccably environmental, miraculously cheap, and if you make a disastrous mess and your creation collapses, you can either use it as kindling or mulch your roses with it, launching yourself with a clear conscience into a new project using tomorrow's papers.

No material is so amenable or adaptable as papier-mâché. In the 19th century, it was used to make

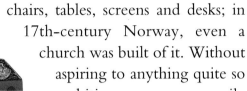

Fish Box
This colorful papier-mâché container is enhanced by three-dimensional molded fish motifs.

chairs, tables, screens and desks; in 17th-century Norway, even a church was built of it. Without aspiring to anything quite so ambitious, you can easily make delicious frivolities like bangles, beads, and brooches, or you can turn your hand to more serious and practical items, such as trays, bowls, and clocks.

As a beginner in a hurry to become acquainted with the stuff, you can enjoy the textured rough-and-ready surface that comes naturally. Cast your mind back to the tactile pleasures and uncritical enthusiasm of kindergarten pursuits: small children lose themselves in the task at hand, whether it be modeling clay men or making palaces of sand – the activity is more absorbing than the finished object – and this is a wonderfully liberating attitude. As you gain experience and can envisage the

Handmade Paper
A rainbow range of colored, speckled paper

creative possibilities of papier-mâché, you can apply an alchemist's repertoire of cunning finishes to emulate the feel and look of lacquer, porcelain, or even marble. You can

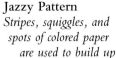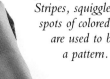

Jazzy Pattern
Stripes, squiggles, and spots of colored paper are used to build up a pattern.

use papier-mâché to explore your long untapped creativity and make a few discoveries about yourself, or you can use it to keep a kitchen full of hyperactive children innocently occupied for a whole rainy weekend.

Papier-mâché can be frisky and naive, or the same humble raw materials can undergo a miraculous transformation and make the smoothest, most subtle, and sophisticated things you have ever seen. Using just a clay base, chicken wire, wooden underpinning, or simply a cardboard frame, you can make some huge and peculiar shapes – such as a pantomime horse, a witch's hat for Halloween night, angels' wings and halos for the annual Christmas nativity play, masks for mardi gras. Alternatively, you can make tiny pieces of jewelry literally in a matter of minutes at the kitchen table, using nothing more arcane than cardboard, paper, paint and glue. You can attack your creation with an electric sander to flatten its bumps, emboss it with string or stitching, distress it, and generally work out your aggression on it. The more refined can dye it, gild it, cover it with baubles, or enchant and embarrass their friends with loving messages using their most calligraphic

Tissue Splendor
Tissue paper painted with metallic powders and oil paints make a decorative napoleon.

Conical Vase
A conical vase is decorated with copper metal leaf, laid onto gold size then rubbed in place.

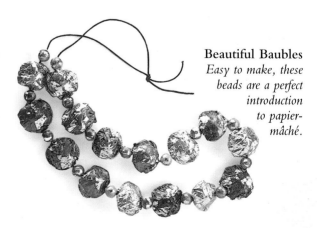

flourishes. You can use tiny glass beads to create a twinkling rim, or big wooden ones attached with thongs of leather to make something that might have come out of Africa. Paper clips and candy wrappers could be recycled to decorate your earrings, or you might develop a penchant for studs or eyelets.

Above all, papier-mâché is good, clean, sticky, innocent fun. Cheap, disposable, and easy to make, you can use it to make the most of vacations and holidays, parades and parties. Celebrate Easter with painted chickens, Christmas with twinkling, gem-studded tree decorations, or a birthday with a brilliant monogrammed box. Papier-mâché is whatever you want to make it – the only limits are those of your imagination. And it is a golden opportunity to regain your lost youth and those evanescent hours in the sandbox. Have fun!

Beautiful Baubles
Easy to make, these beads are a perfect introduction to papier-mâché.

Basic Materials and Equipment

PAPIER-MACHE is an extemely cheap pastime because its principal material is recycled newspaper. Many of the other basic materials and items of equipment you will need to get started – such as scissors, glue, cardboard, masking tape, pencils, and crayons – can be found around the home. Other pieces of equipment you will find useful include a craft knife and cutting mat, chicken wire, and modeling clay. Once you progress from the beginner stage and want to experiment with different finishes and decorations, there are a few things you will have to purchase, but these are not

Assorted paper

Craft knife and blade

Scissors

◀ **Paper Selection**
This is the essential ingredient for papier-mâché; you can use newsprint, plain white sketch paper, or even brown paper for making pulp and layering, or colored papers for a more decorative finish. You could also decorate your finished papier-mâché with a selection of stylish patterned paper.

▲ **Cutting Tools**
A pair of sharp scissors and a lethally sharp craft knife are required for accurate cutting of cardboard to make frameworks. Be careful when using a craft knife, and always use a cutting mat.

Wallpaper paste

Rabbit-skin glue granules

▶ **Glues and Fixings**
Use wallpaper paste or polyvinyl glue for pasting on paper strips or for mixing with soaked paper to make paper pulp. Rabbit-skin glue is an ingredient in gilding. Masking tape is used for reinforcing joints, and for attaching cardboard pieces together to make a framework.

Polyvinyl white glue

Metal ruler

Masking tape

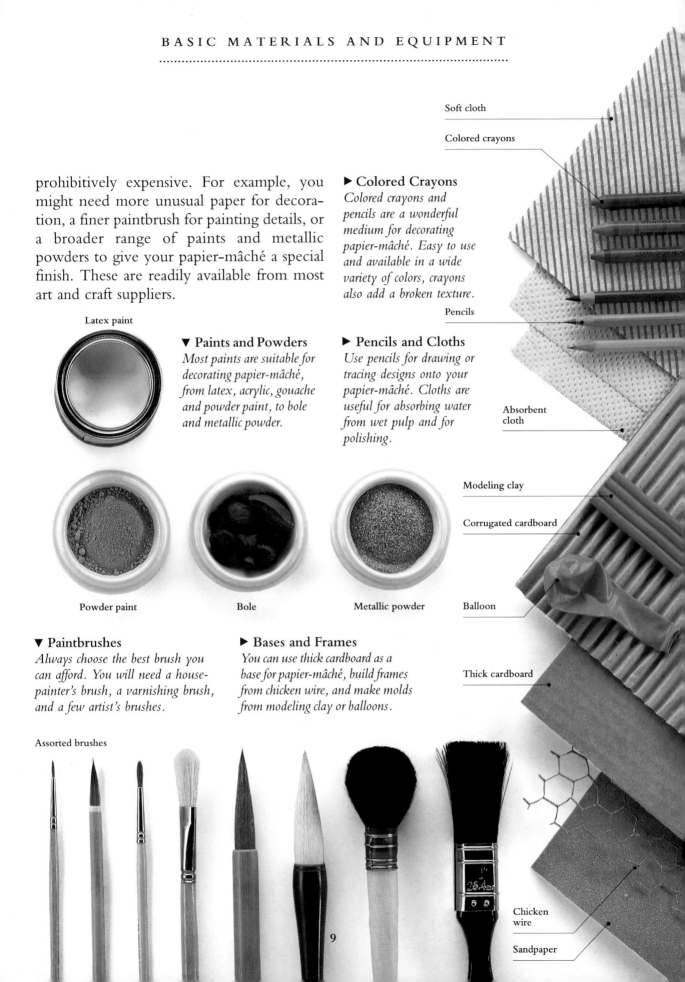

prohibitively expensive. For example, you might need more unusual paper for decoration, a finer paintbrush for painting details, or a broader range of paints and metallic powders to give your papier-mâché a special finish. These are readily available from most art and craft suppliers.

Soft cloth

Colored crayons

▶ Colored Crayons
Colored crayons and pencils are a wonderful medium for decorating papier-mâché. Easy to use and available in a wide variety of colors, crayons also add a broken texture.

Pencils

Latex paint

▼ Paints and Powders
Most paints are suitable for decorating papier-mâché, from latex, acrylic, gouache and powder paint, to bole and metallic powder.

▶ Pencils and Cloths
Use pencils for drawing or tracing designs onto your papier-mâché. Cloths are useful for absorbing water from wet pulp and for polishing.

Absorbent cloth

Modeling clay

Corrugated cardboard

Powder paint

Bole

Metallic powder

Balloon

▼ Paintbrushes
Always choose the best brush you can afford. You will need a house-painter's brush, a varnishing brush, and a few artist's brushes.

▶ Bases and Frames
You can use thick cardboard as a base for papier-mâché, build frames from chicken wire, and make molds from modeling clay or balloons.

Thick cardboard

Assorted brushes

Chicken wire

Sandpaper

Getting Started

THE BEST THING about papier-mâché is that you can start right now. You don't need complicated equipment, expensive materials, or a degree in fine arts to begin. Mistakes don't matter one bit, and while perfection is a laudable ambition, it is by no means essential – you can turn out a very respectable and charming bowl while you are getting the hang of the process. As your confidence grows, you can proceed to more demanding shapes and more exacting finishes.

To start with, nothing beats speed. Kick off with something that you can finish today. A tiny trinket bowl to learn about the different properties of layered paper and pulp, an angular vase that builds on a straightforward cardboard shape – these are the simple first principles from which all else follows. So put on your oldest shirt, forget the ironing, and enjoy your paperwork.

Tissue Scraps

MATERIALS

2 pieces 33 × 23½in
(84 × 60cm)
sketch paper
Water
Polyvinyl white glue
Plastic wrap

EQUIPMENT

Large bowl
Blender
Sieve
Cloth

See p.15 for materials
to decorate the bowl.

P APIER-MACHE is nothing if not adaptable – by using different techniques you can be bright and bold, or subtle and refined. This little bowl made of decorated pulp is at the more ethereal end of the spectrum, and exploits the delicate translucency of tissue paper with a confetti of tiny overlapping pieces speckled with gold, echoing the discreetly shimmering haze of gold, bronze, and turquoise on the outside.

Once the potential of paper as a decorative material in its own right takes hold, you will see possibilities in the most unlikely places: different colors and qualities of tissue paper and fine handmade paper combine to give a different effect; natural wheat and straw colors mixed with gold and black speckles look very sophisticated, while more layers of blues and greens give depth and brilliance. Or you might use printed tissue as a collage, with decorative citrus fruit wrappers, the blue and white pictorial papers favored by some French bakers to show off their baguettes, or bought tissue covered in extravagant blowsy roses – all torn into tiny pieces and attached to your bowl in an intricate jigsaw of abstract pattern.

Translucent Tissue
Tissue paper scraps layered in this bowl have the luminous translucency of a wash of watercolor paint. This is a fascinating way to exploit the huge range of newly available handmade dyed and textured papers. The interplay of technique and color within and outside makes this bowl something of a subtle work of art.

Going for Gold
These two shimmering gold bowls achieve two different effects: for ultimate dazzle go for gold; to soften the effect decorate with tissue pieces for a bowl of beautiful scraps.

Making the Bowl

*Paper pulp gives a very different texture than layering –
the even roughness has a tactile charm. A certain effort is
necessary to give the pulp a regular thickness.*

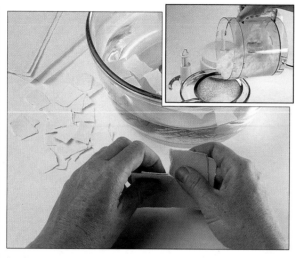

1 *Tear the pieces of sketch paper into small pieces about
1in (2.5cm) square and soak overnight in a bowl of
water. Taking a handful at a time and adding plenty of
water, liquify the soaked paper in a blender to make pulp.
Strain the paper pulp to remove excess water (see inset).
The resulting pulp should be a spongy mass.*

2 *Add polyvinyl glue to the sieved pulp in the
proportion of approximately 2 tbsp (1oz/30g)
polyvinyl glue to 2 cups (1lb/500g) paper pulp. Mix the
glue in with your hands until it is incorporated. The pulp
mixture should now be spongy and silky to the touch.*

3 *Line your bowl with plastic wrap and press a few
handfuls of pulp into its base with the back of your
fingers to compress the fibers and remove any air pockets.
Build up the sides of the bowl, pressing with a dry cloth as
you go (see inset) to remove excess water, until the pulp
feels hard and damp to the touch. Make sure the thickness
of the bowl is even all around.*

4 *After letting the pressed pulp dry in a warm place for a
few hours, gently ease away the plastic wrap from the
edges of the mold. Carefully lift out the damp paper bowl
and peel away the plastic wrap. If any cracks or holes
appear in the paper bowl, fill them in with damp pulp and
smooth this over with your fingers. Leave the bowl to dry
completely for a few days.*

Decorating the Bowl

Tiny, overlapping postage stamps of subtly colored tissue decorate the inside of this gilded bowl, a translucent finish that is just right for such a delicate and fragile creation.

Decorated tissue paper

MATERIALS
Iridescent acrylic
paints
Nontarnishing
wax gilt
Tissue paper
Gold ink
Polyvinyl white glue
Metallic powder
Water

EQUIPMENT
Artist's brush
Cloth
Protective mask

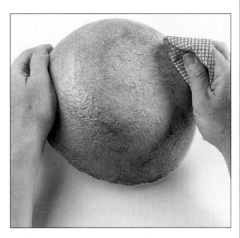

1 *Coat the inside of the bowl with a thin layer of iridescent white acrylic paint, and the outside with a thin layer of bronze. The paints will soak in and seal all the surfaces. Allow the paints to dry. Then, using a combination of pale gold, bronze and turquoise, paint the outside in a random manner and let dry for an hour.*

2 *Dip a soft dry cloth into nontarnishing wax gilt, then rub it gently over the outside of the bowl. This will give the bowl a soft sheen.*

3 *Decorate pieces of tissue paper with dye or paint and let dry. Then spatter the paper with gold ink. First dip a brush in gold ink. Then, holding the brush over the paper, tap it against your hand to produce fine spatters, or flick the brush over the paper to produce larger spots. Finally, dab the brush randomly over the paper to produce large blobs. Let dry.*

4 *Tear the tissue paper into small pieces, approximately 1in (2.5cm) square. Using a diluted mixture of 1 part polyvinyl glue to 1 part water, coat the inside of the bowl, then stick down overlapping pieces of tissue. Paste more diluted glue on top of the tissue to seal. Then paste tissue pieces randomly in the same manner on the outside of the bowl. Allow the bowl to dry.*

5 *Paint polyvinyl glue around the rim of the bowl and in the center of the tissue paper squares on the outside of the bowl. Dust lightly with metallic powder. It is advisable to wear a mask to reduce the risk of inhaling the fine metallic powder.*

Tiny Starburst Bowl

MATERIALS

1 piece 33 × 23½ in (84 × 60cm) sketch paper
Water
Cold water fiber-reactive dyes
Plastic wrap
Shellac (optional)

EQUIPMENT

Bowl
Blender
Sieve
3 small dishes
Spoon
Cloth
Varnish brush

THIS LITTLE JEWEL-LIKE BOWL is unusual in that the bold colors on the inside and outside of the bowl correspond with each other exactly. In terms of papier-mâché, you cannot get much simpler than this formula, and the pulp technique is not difficult to master. The result has great charm, with its intense depth of color and blurred bands of pattern.

Working with pulp gives an opportunity to experiment with different dyes, both subtle and bright, or the pastel shades that result from using colored papers. Small pieces of gold foil or thread can be incorporated in the process to give a finish of glittering richness, while a final coat of varnish will seal and protect the finished bowl and intensify the color.

Little bowls like this look very pretty in groups – each one slightly different in color, pattern, and size from its neighbor. They make the perfect containers to cheer up and organize desk or dressing table paraphernalia. Like all papier-mâché, they do not appreciate being wet – they would look very pretty in a fresh modern bathroom, but need several coats of varnish first to make sure they do not disintegrate.

Stars and Flowers
This pretty, feather-light bowl is built up from sketch paper pulped in a blender and richly colored with cold-water fabric dye. This technique is unique because the pattern and color are integral to the bowl and identical inside and out. The finished result has a lighthearted delicacy that could not be achieved by any other method.

Speckles, Stars, and Spirals
Professional dyes produce the most intense color, while commercial fabric dyes give a softer effect. You could omit the dyeing stage and use colored paper, which results in muted pastel colors.

Making the Bowl

Construction and decoration are part of the same process in this tiny, vibrant bowl. Nimble fingers and patience are necessary to keep colors separate and the pattern distinct.

1 *Tear the piece of sketch paper first into narrow strips and then into small pieces about 1in (2.5cm) square, and soak overnight in a bowl of water. This amount of paper will produce enough pulp to make three small bowls.*

2 *Add a handful of soaked paper to a blender and, adding plenty of water, liquify the paper to make pulp. It may take a little while to liquify all the paper because it is best to add only one handful of paper at a time, to avoid overloading the blender. Strain the paper pulp to remove excess water. The resulting pulp should resemble a spongy mass.*

3 *Divide the pulp into three containers. Prepare cold-water fiber-reactive dyes in yellow, pink, and blue, following the manufacturer's instructions. Add drops of dye to each portion of pulp, mixing in well with a spoon. Let soak for several hours, then rinse the pulp well. (If you prefer, you could use colored papers to make the pulp and omit the dyeing stage. However, the colors will be less intense.)*

4 *Line a bowl with plastic wrap. This will serve as the mold. Using a teaspoon, carefully arrange spoonfuls of yellow and pink pulp in the base of the mold to create a flower design. Then press the pulp gently with your fingertips to compress it and remove any air pockets.*

5 *Add spoonfuls of blue pulp to the mold to extend the design up the sides of the mold. As the pulp is quite sticky, it will cling to the sides of the mold and keep its shape. Keep turning the mold around as you add the pulp, so you can see the design from all sides. Continue to press the pulp gently with your fingertips or a teaspoon as you work.*

6 *Add more layers of pink and yellow pulp. Then, using a clean dry cloth, press the pulp carefully to compact the fibers and soak up the excess water collecting in the bottom of the bowl. Do not press too hard in case the pulp comes away from the sides of the mold. Repair any small gaps that may appear with pieces of pulp. Similarly, if a blob of pulp falls onto pulp of a different color, simply remove it and patch up the design with the matching color.*

7 *Continue adding pulp to build up the design until you reach the rim of the bowl. Then, using another dry cloth, press the pulp as hard as you can, working your way around the bowl, until the pulp feels hard and no longer wet.*

8 *Leave the bowl in a warm place, such as a sunny windowsill, to dry for a few hours. Then carefully ease away the plastic wrap from the sides of the mold and lift out the paper bowl.*

9 *Peel away the plastic wrap from the outside of the bowl and let the bowl dry out completely for a few days. Then, if you like, you can varnish it with shellac to deepen the colors.*

Brilliant Fishes

MATERIALS

Newsprint
Petroleum jelly
Polyvinyl white glue
Water
Dishwashing liquid
Modeling clay
Tissue paper
White latex paint

EQUIPMENT

Dish to act as
mold
Cloth
Scissors
Cake rack
Scalpel
Craft knife
Paintbrush

See p.23 for materials
to decorate the dish.

THE SIZZLING, high-intensity color of this dish is a result of using opaque gouache paints. Gouache is an amiable medium and lends itself to crisp detail and sharply defined decoration. Easily built up in the classic fashion from many layers of paper, the sturdy solidity of this dish is enlivened by a three-dimensional sprinkling of shells. The more astrologically inclined might undertake a firmament of stars and moons, but there are many other simple and fashionable decorative motifs that can be adapted to add interest to an otherwise plain shape.

Layered papier-mâché is justly renowned for its lightness and strength. Once you have created large oval and circular dishes, you might try a tray based on an existing plastic version. The Victorians excelled in the fine art of papier-mâché, and produced ornately shaped "parlor-maid" trays to which they applied finely painted or decoupaged flowers, layers of lacquer, or lustrous pieces of abalone shell. Experiment and be inventive with your decoration.

Fin Extraordinaire
Wild subaqueous psychedelia with strange rainbow fishes and speckled shells cavorts on a purple and burgundy background freckled with gold. Opaque gouache paint allows the finest detail of fin and gill to be perfectly delineated.

Bowled Over
Anyone can manage quiet good taste – but accomplished kitsch is a much more exacting art. This bold and brilliant bowl is an exercise in unabashed extroversion, its entire surface richly decorated with skill and finesse.

Making the Dish

A simple shape brought to life with three-dimensional decorations molded with modeling clay. It would be possible to use real shells if sculpting is beyond you.

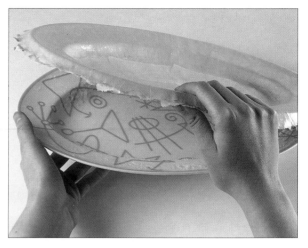

1 *Tear strips of newsprint about 2in (5cm) long. Rub a generous layer of petroleum jelly over the surface of the dish. Then, using diluted polyvinyl glue (3 parts glue to 1 part water), paste on strips of paper, overlapping as you go. Repeat the process, applying about 15 layers in all. Let dry for 48 hours.*

2 *Carefully ease back the rim of the paper dish, working your way around the edge, and peel it away from the mold. Clean the underside with a soft cloth and dish-washing liquid to remove all traces of petroleum jelly. Trim the edges of the dish with scissors, following the line of the rim on the underside.*

3 *Make three shells out of modeling clay, each approximately 2in (5cm) long and 1in (2.5m) wide, or to fit the rim. On each shell, rub petroleum jelly over one side at a time and, using diluted polyvinyl glue, paste several layers of tissue paper over the surface. Let dry and repeat the process until you have built up about 30 layers.*

4 *After leaving the shells to dry on a cake rack for 48 hours, cut each shell in half with a craft knife. Scoop out the modeling clay with a small knife – it should come out easily if plenty of petroleum jelly was used earlier. Scrape out any remaining modeling clay to leave the paper shell halves clean.*

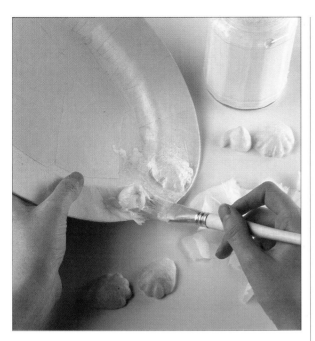

5 Using diluted polyvinyl glue, glue the paper shell halves onto the rim of the paper dish. Hold the shells in position for a few minutes until they are secure. Then paste three layers of tissue paper over the shell shapes and leave to dry overnight.

6 Apply a coat of white latex paint over the entire dish and leave to dry. This will provide a smooth surface for decorating.

Decorating the Dish

A thick coat of latex paint – the poor man's gesso – smooths out the paper edges and makes a good surface for precise gouache fish of unknown species. Copy designs for fish, birds, or butterflies from nature books.

MATERIALS	EQUIPMENT
Gouache paints	Artist's brush
Spray varnish	Pencil
Gloss interior wood varnish	Tracing paper

Using gouache paints, paint a fish design onto the dish. If you do not feel confident enough in your freehand skills, find suitable images in a book and, having photocopied them to the desired size, transfer them onto the dish with tracing or carbon paper. Paint the background in blue gouache to represent the sea, then paint each fish in a variety of bright colors. Paint the rim in a contrasting color and finally paint the shells. Let dry, then apply one coat of spray varnish to set the gouache. Finally, paint on two thin coats of gloss interior wood varnish for a tough shiny surface, allowing the varnish to dry between coats.

Tricorn Vase

MATERIALS
Thin cardboard
Mat board
Masking tape
Wallpaper paste
Newsprint
Pre-mixed filler

EQUIPMENT
Pencil
Tracing paper
Cutting mat
Metal ruler
Craft knife
Teaspoon

See p.27 for materials
to decorate the vase.

CRISP, ELEGANT ANGULAR LINES give this vase a sculptural quality. It has no affinity with fluffy flowers: if its contents have to be floral, spiky dried eryngium heads would be suitable or, alternatively, skeletal twigs, festooned with a string of tiny white electric lights for an unsentimental nod to Christmas.

One advantage of a surface of flat planes is that it is ideal for collage – photocopied musical scores, possibly dipped in tea for fake antiquity, have the right kind of graphic appeal.

The artist who designed this vase has applied science – or geometry at least – to achieve more ambitious projects, such as a handsome fire screen with mantelpiece and a gilded three-legged table. Both have an air of theatrical panache, and, while the former might be a fire hazard and the latter might not withstand heavy loads, they dramatically expand the repertoire of paper and glue.

Verdigris Vase
Using a geometric cardboard base gives this vase a strong masculine look unusual with papier-mâché. Its bronzy verdigris finish would be perfectly at home with modern furniture in a cool, uncluttered interior.

Graphic Appeal
The flat planes of the basic shape make an ideal surface to show off photocopied images and text in a graphic black-and-white collage. Or black and silver can be paired for sophistication.

Making the Vase

*A geometric approach to the imprecise art of papier-mâché,
carefully cut and scored mat board gives an unusually
decisive shape, in contrast to the more usual irregularities.*

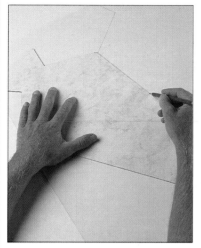

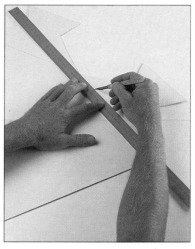

1 *Enlarge the template on p.92 to the required size, trace it onto thin cardboard, and cut it out. Draw around the template three times on mat board, with the long sides of the template placed next to each other, so that you have one penciled shape.*

2 *Place the mat board on a cutting mat and, using a metal ruler and a scalpel or craft knife, carefully cut around the outline of the penciled shape.*

3 *Draw a pencil line along the base of the vase neck and, using a craft knife and metal ruler, score along these lines to make them easier to fold and give a sharper crease. Score along the side edges of the vase in the same way.*

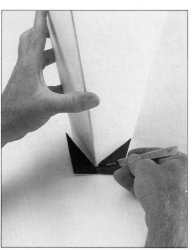

4 *Turn the mat board over and score along the narrow part of the vase neck in the same way as before. Mat board with a black underside is recommended because a dark interior will give the vase a more finished look.*

5 *Fold the sides of the vase in to make a three-sided shape and tape together with masking tape. Bend in the folds of the neck and then tape these together. Aim for a close fit, but slight inaccuracies do not matter at this stage.*

6 *Place the constructed vase on cardboard and cut around the edges to make a base. Tape the base to the bottom of the vase.*

7 *Using wallpaper paste, paste 6 × 3in (15 × 7.5cm) strips of newsprint or brown paper over the vase to cover it entirely. Allow to dry, then repeat with another layer of paper strips. Let dry overnight. It is best not to use smaller strips of paper than these, as they will make the mat board frame soggy and possibly misshapen, and create more lines on the finished vase.*

8 *Mix up a small amount of premixed filler following the manufacturer's instructions, then insert two tablespoonfuls inside the vase to weight the base and help the vase stand upright. Check that the filler drops to the base and does not stick to the sides of the vase — if it does stick to the sides, simply shake the vase until the filler drops down to the base.*

Decorating the Vase
Tinting latex paint produces some extraordinary luminous colors. Here the gilding emphasizes the edges of the paper strips, and the coat of shoe polish and bronze tones down the turquoise and gold.

Bronze powder

Shoe polish

MATERIALS
White latex paint
Phthalo green acrylic paint
Shoe polish
Bronze powder
Hair spray

EQUIPMENT
Housepainter's brush
Cloth

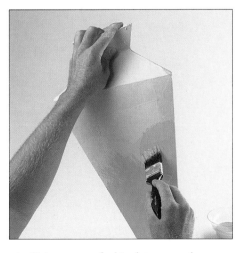

1 *Paint a coat of white latex over the papered vase. Leave to dry and then apply a coat of phthalo green acrylic paint mixed with white latex. Here the color was obtained by mixing 1 part acrylic paint with 2 parts latex paint. Leave the painted vase to dry thoroughly.*

2 *Dip a soft cloth first in shoe polish and then in bronze powder. Then smear it quickly and lightly over the dry painted surface of the vase to leave random bronze patches over the vase, with the green color still showing through. To set the bronze powder, spray the vase with hair spray.*

Opalescent Bowl

MATERIALS

Cardboard
Balloon
String
Newsprint
Polyvinyl white glue
Water
Sawdust
Whiting
Linseed oil
Wallpaper paste
White latex paint, casein, or gesso

EQUIPMENT

Plate, or pair of compasses
Scissors
Craft knife
Flowerpot
Housepainter's brush
Bowl

See p.31 for materials to decorate the bowl.

E VERYONE LIKES BOWLS. There is something rotundly satisfying about the shape, and they can be modeled upon existing bowls, balloons, or even soccer balls. The basic shape can be played with in a variety of ways to make a rounded, egg-shaped, or cylindrical body, with a ragged or smooth edge and a splayed or crimped lip. Decorate your bowl with string patterns, silver foil, silver studs, faux jewels, or other *objets trouvés,* and stand it on three globular feet or a solid base made from a collar of cardboard.

Having done all this, you can launch into the surface decoration of your bowl. Texture comes from glass-smooth gesso or the rustic rasp of sawdust. Color can be solidly matte, or you can use layers of transparent inks or pearlized paint for a swirling, nacreous quality. You can add gold leaf, folksy potato prints or precise penlines, and give it an ancient air with antiquing or crackle varnish. In fact, life can be a bowl of just about anything you desire.

Metallic Effect
Black ink makes its opalescent heart gleam darkly, almost like pewter; flakes and shreds of leaf metal are scattered about its collar, and dark aquamarine matte paint is buffed to bring out its full intensity around the outside of this quirky and appealing bowl.

Bowl of Contrasts
As fragile as a peony and as tough as leather, the delicate gilded exterior of this bowl contrasts dramatically with the powerful orange-red coloring inside.

28

Making the Bowl

A quick and easy way to make a footed bowl. Use pulp thickened with sawdust for a deliberately irregular organic look, enhanced by the undulating rim.

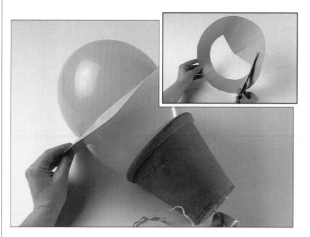

1 Using a plate or pair of compasses, cut a circle out of cardboard the required diameter of the outer rim. Cut a cross in the center with a craft knife, then cut out the inner circle (see inset). Blow up a balloon inside the rim and tie a knot in the end. Fasten with a length of string and thread it through the hole in the base of an earthenware flowerpot for support.

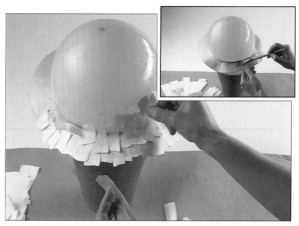

2 Having torn the newsprint into small pieces, cover the balloon and rim with polyvinyl glue (see inset). Apply a line of pieces along one third of the outer edge of the rim. Then work up over the rim and to the top of the balloon in overlapping rows. Repeat this process until the surface of the balloon is completely covered.

3 Paint glue generously over the balloon and rim, smoothing from top to bottom to expel air bubbles. Repeat the layering and gluing to build up three or four layers. Hang the bowl up by the string in a warm place – it will take about one hour to dry over a warm oven. As it dries, the rim will get wavy. Pop the balloon and remove it from the bowl.

4 To make paper pulp, tear up four double sheets of newsprint and make into pulp, as in steps 1 and 2 on p.18. Add an equal part sawdust, ½ part whiting, 3 cups polyvinyl glue and 2 tablespoons linseed oil. Mix and sprinkle the wallpaper paste on top to absorb excess moisture. Apply the pulp evenly over the inside and rim of the bowl, smoothing it out well with wet fingers.

5 *Dry the bowl in a cool oven. Cut a narrow strip of cardboard and glue or tape the ends together to make a small circle. Place this on the bottom of the bowl and fill with pulp, pressing down evenly.*

6 *When dry, trim the excess paper from the rim with scissors and paint the bowl inside and out with white latex paint, casein paint, or gesso.*

Decorating the Bowl

Pearlized acrylic ink is used here to give a glowing, translucent effect, heightened by gold metal leaf on the rim.

Gold metal leaf

MATERIALS
Pale turquoise
pearlized acrylic ink
Darker turquoise
transparent acrylic ink
Diluted black ink
Polyurethane varnish
Gold metal leaf
Beeswax

EQUIPMENT
Artist's brush
Paper towels
Cloth

1 *Cover the inside and rim of the bowl with pale turquoise pearlized ink. When dry, paint darker turquoise ink on the outside and streak it over the rim.*

2 *Rub diluted black ink on the inside of the bowl, then rub down the outside and inside with crumpled paper towels for a distressed effect.*

3 *Paint the rim with varnish and, when touch-dry, apply gold metal leaf torn into small pieces. Rub down with the ball of the thumb or a crumpled paper towel. Finally, polish the bowl with a cloth dipped in beeswax to build up a protective patina.*

Well Urned

MATERIALS

Newsprint
Water
Polyvinyl white glue
Wallpaper paste
Linseed oil
Petroleum jelly
Masking tape
White latex paint
Acrylic and metallic paints
Colored crayons
Fixative
Satin spray varnish

EQUIPMENT

Large bowl
Blender
Sieve
Garden urn for mold
Craft knife
Housepainter's brush
Artist's brush

PAPIER–MACHE HAS MANY VIRTUES – it is lightweight, cheap, durable and adaptable. It can be used to make tiny beads and huge containers equally successfully – and even if you do have a complete disaster and your work of art collapses in a heap of pulp, you can, toss it out and start again with a clear conscience. So do not be afraid to tackle sizeable objects, such as this beautiful urn. As long as you have something to act as a mold, there is nothing to stop you. Here the shape was taken from a garden urn; the layered paper and pulp were carefully cut away in two halves and then stuck together again – a perfectly respectable method that allows you to make use of more complex shapes and to explore life beyond the bowl. Try using existing vases, bottles, lamp bases, and candlesticks as molds – narrow necks are not a problem. If you are feeling particularly creative, you might experiment with a lamp base (weighted with dried beans for stability) and give it a matching shade.

Colourful Trio
Handsome containers for walking sticks and umbrellas or the perfect receptacles for fake sunflowers, this trio of sunny-colored urns look good together as variations on a theme. Make sure that the bases are weighted and very thoroughly sealed if they are likely to get damp.

1 *Make paper pulp (see p.13) using 12 sheets of newsprint, 8 tablespoons polyvinyl glue, and 2 teaspoons each of wallpaper paste and linseed oil. Cover the sides of the mold with petroleum jelly, then with newsprint. When dry, smooth on pulp, ½ in (1cm) thick. Dry for a week, then repeat for the base.*

2 *Using a sharp craft knife, cut the molded pulp in half down the length of the urn. Gently ease one pulp half away from the mold. You might find it helpful to use a spatula here. If any pieces of pulp break off, don't despair – simply stick them back in place with polyvinyl glue.*

3 *Glue the pulp halves together using polyvinyl glue. Wrap masking tape around the outside to secure. Paste two layers of newsprint dipped in diluted polyvinyl glue over the urn. When dry, paint it with white latex, then decorate with paint and crayons (see p.51), and when dry, spray with fixative and varnish.*

Ideas to Inspire

Shown on the following pages is a range of papier-mâché bowls and plates – all different in style, shape, design and size – to inspire the budding artist. Now that you have learned the basics of making a bowl, experiment with some of the ideas suggested here; alternatively, take a molding technique from one, add a clever use of beads from another, and make something that is truly, inimitably, your own.

▶ **A Class Menagerie**
Made from paper pulp using a bowl as a mold, these bowls take the theme of animals and birds. Simple shapes are repeated around the inside, decorated with acrylics and crayon over a painted base, while the rims are highlighted in gold.

▼ **Jagged Edges**
Jagged cardboard rims were taped to the bowl edges and held in place with glued paper. The bowls were coated with a white latex/polyvinyl glue mix, then painted in blue and orange acrylics and decorated with ripped paper.

▼ Sunflower Bowl
Made from layering paper over a mold and taping on irregular cardboard shapes for the petals, this bowl was painted with acrylic paints and decorated with torn circles of paper and ink to create the sunflower seeds.

▲ Starfish Plate
The starfish shapes were painted gold, and the plate was decorated with torn paper, painted green, then spattered with gold.

▶ **Patchwork Bowls**
*Inspired by Aboriginal art, these bowls were made from
pulp using a cardboard mold; the feet, consisting of a
trio of marble-sized balls of pulp, were attached
with glue. The bowls were decorated with gouache
and watercolors, with gold leaf around the rim,
and the spiral was decorated with
candy wrappers.*

◀ **Gilded Bowls**
*The crusty edge to these
bowls was formed by leaving the wet
pulp ragged at the rim. The bowls
were painted inside and out with
iridescent acrylics, and the rims were
decorated with gold leaf. Finally, parts of
both the inside and outside of the bowls
were also decorated with gold leaf.*

▲ African Inspiration
*Made from pulp, colored
only by the newsprint and construction
paper used to make it, these bowls
were pressed into plaster molds to create an
ethnic pattern. The addition of chunky, wooden
beads around the rim, attached with threading twine
through holes drilled in the papier-mâché, completes
your own personal tribal artifact.*

Shaping, Molding, and Frameworks

· ·

H AVING MASTERED THE BASICS and built up an impressive collection of bowls, you may want to make something a little more grand and altogether more challenging. Papier-mâché is a miraculously versatile medium. It can be built up over a wire base to make three-dimensional sculptures; it can be layered over a cardboard shape for strength and texture; you can shape it over metal, ceramic, plastic, or plaster; or you can shape it like clay to make your own version of baroque moldings. Once you have explored its possibilities, nothing will be safe from a thorough papering. With a little chicken wire or a sheet of cardboard, you can conquer the third dimension.

Jazz-Time Clock

MATERIALS
Double corrugated
cardboard
Polyvinyl white glue
Wallpaper paste
Paper

EQUIPMENT
Pair of compasses
Pencil
Scissors
Craft knife
Cutting mat
Paintbrush

See p.43 for materials
to decorate the clock.

TIMES HAVE CHANGED since the family grandfather clock ruled the hours. Clock mechanisms are now easy to come by and ridiculously cheap, so that you can design a different clock for every room in the house, or make a special-occasion clock to commemorate a golden anniversary or a 21st birthday.

Your clock can be any shape you wish. You might want something grand to grace your living-room mantelpiece – columns, perhaps, with a square marbled face and discreet gilding. For your bedroom, disporting cherubs, photocopied and decoupaged, might help you to wake with a smile on your face.

Clock numerals do not need to be spelled out: you could time your soufflé by a clock whose hands are carrots and whose numerals are radishes, or your hours can be marked by shells or sequins, autumn leaves, or numbers photocopied from typeface catalogs or torn from newspapers.

Rose Window Clock Face
Strong, glowing colors, as bright as a stained glass window, enliven a clock face that has brilliantly transcended its humble origins. Indigo, purple, magenta, cerulean blue, and fir green are not chosen for discretion, but for fun. Zigzags, spots, stars: papier-mâché is a blank canvas upon which to experiment, and an invitation to have a good time.

New Faces
Anything with a flat front can become a clock – a circle, triangle, or square. You can stand it on little feet and use Victorian engravings or gift wrap as decoration if your design skills fail you.

Making the Clock

A classy way to recycle old cardboard boxes, extravagantly layered
in three chunky dimensions. Precision cutting is helpful, but not
essential, and you can change size and shape to suit your whim.

1 *Using a pair of compasses, draw four circles*
approximately 6in (15cm) in diameter on a piece of
double corrugated cardboard. In the center of three of these
circles draw another circle, measuring approximately 4in
(10cm) in diameter.

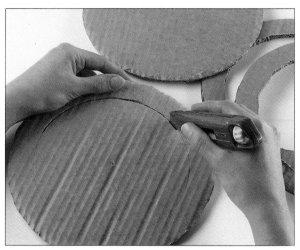

2 *Cut out all four circles from the cardboard, then cut out*
the inner circles from three of these circles. It is easiest
to use scissors to cut the outer circles, and a craft knife to
cut the inner circles. When using a craft knife, protect your
work surface with a cutting mat.

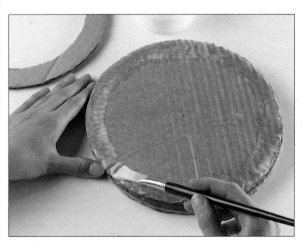

3 *Pasting polyvinyl glue between layers, sandwich the*
four circles together in the following order: two cut-
out circles, one solid circle, then one cut-out circle. Place a
heavy weight on top of the glued circles, and let dry for
about two hours.

4 *Mix the wallpaper paste according to the*
manufacturer's instructions. Tear paper into strips
approximately 2in (5cm) long and 1in (2.5cm) wide. Dip
the strips one at a time into the wallpaper paste and paste
the strips onto the "clock," smoothing them with your
fingers. Overlap the layers as you go, and apply two layers
on both sides of the clock before letting it dry.

Decorating the Clock

Colored paper comes in an irresistible rainbow range and has a pleasant speckled texture — all of which you can exploit to the fullest, with lively additional spots and squiggles of your own.

Colored medium-
weight paper

MATERIALS
Polyvinyl white glue
Colored medium-
weight paper
Water-based gloss
varnish
Clock movement and
hands
Quick-acting epoxy
resin adhesive

EQUIPMENT
Wooden skewer or
toothpick
Drill

1 *Using diluted polyvinyl glue (2 parts glue to 1 part water), paste small overlapping strips of colored paper onto the top and underside of the clock to cover the base completely.*

2 *Cut circles out of the colored paper and paste these in a random pattern over the base on the front of the clock. There is no need to let the base dry first.*

3 *Paste on pieces of different-colored paper to build up the pattern. Use a wooden skewer to hold narrow strips of paper in place. Here triangles and small circles have been decorated with squiggles and dots. Leave the clock to dry overnight. Then apply a coat of water-based gloss varnish to protect the surface.*

4 *Turn the clock over so that the decorated side faces downward and drill a hole in the center of the clock back large enough to accommodate the shaft of the clock movement. Glue the clock movement in place with epoxy resin adhesive applied both to the clock mechanism and to the back of the clock.*

5 *Cover the clock hands with colored paper by pasting polyvinyl glue onto the clock hands and placing them on a piece of colored paper. Tear the paper around the hands, fold the torn paper edges over the back and glue them down to secure. Finally, attach the clock hands to the shaft of the clock movement and screw the center piece over the hands to fasten.*

Curtained Mirror

MATERIALS

Plastic sheet
Mirror
Chicken wire
Picture-hanging wire
Newsprint
Wallpaper paste
White photocopy
paper

EQUIPMENT

Wire cutters
Ruler

See p.47 for materials
to decorate the
mirror frame.

A STUNNING EXAMPLE of the dramatic potential to be found in humble chicken wire and newsprint, this piece of trompe-l'oeil displays – besides your face – a wonderful vigorous humor. Such a frame could cheer your outlook on the grayest Monday morning.

Building the design up with a photocopier gives you unlimited possibilities: you could use pages from Leonardo da Vinci's notebook, repeated images of fleurs-de-lis, or botanical engravings culled from a graphic sourcebook. Enlarging and reducing, darkening and refining motifs gives them an interesting quality. If you have access to a color photocopier, the visual world is yours to exploit. You could make a personal design from a collage of your past using gift wrap, valentines, postcards, ribbons, pressed flowers, and skeleton leaves. Or you could base a freehand design on the elegant intricacies of Elizabethan embroidery. Once you start looking, you will see inspiration everywhere.

Tapestry Effect
A fabulous fake: newspaper and chicken wire drapery that falls in the extravagant folds of a piece of medieval tapestry – an effect that rich colors, bold patterns, and matte varnish would emphasize.

Material Differences
Bronze, gold, chocolate brown, and cinnabar – warm rich colors for a candlelit mirror that exploits the sculptural possibilities of chicken wire.

Making the Mirror Frame

A wire armature enables you to create whatever sculptural shape inspires you – and because of the lightness and low cost of the materials, size is no problem.

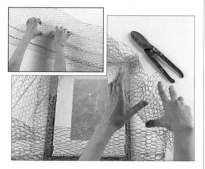

1 *Tape a plastic sheet over the mirror to protect it. Cut a piece of chicken wire larger than the mirror. This mirror is 15 × 10in (38 × 25cm) and the wire 36 × 18in (90 × 45cm). Lay the mirror on top of the wire so that it is 14in (33cm) from the bottom. Fold up the lower edge of the wire over the mirror base by ½ in (1cm), then fold it back toward you to hold the mirror base. Fold the wire underneath itself to make a shelf at the base of the mirror.*

2 *Using wire cutters, make a cut into both sides of the chicken wire at the top and bottom edge of the mirror. Fold the wire in toward the mirror on each side, then fold it back out after securing the mirror by ½ in (1cm). Repeat with the top edge of the mirror and tuck under the wire ends to neaten.*

3 *Cut out another piece of chicken wire measuring 52 × 18in (130 × 45cm) for the drape, and bunch it into loose folds along its entire length (see inset). Arrange the wire drape around the mirror, pulling and manipulating it into shape. When you are satisfied with its appearance, secure it in position around the mirror by snipping individual wires along its length and folding them around the base wire.*

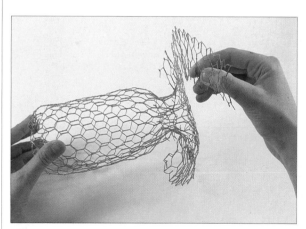

4 *To make the vase, cut a piece of wire measuring 9¼ × 10½in (23 × 26cm) and roll it into a cylinder shape. Tuck the wire ends under at the base of the cylinder and fold the ends back slightly at the top to make the vase neck. Cut another piece of wire measuring 18 × 2in (45 × 5cm) for the rim and attach this to the neck of the cylinder shape. Secure it to the shelf of the mirror frame. Then attach a piece of picture-hanging wire to the back of the mirror frame.*

5 *Using large squares of newsprint dipped in wallpaper paste, cover the front of the wire frame with a layer of newsprint, smoothing the paper down as you go. Repeat with a layer of white photocopy paper. When pasting paper strips next to the mirror, paste the paper to the mirror to secure it in place. Allow the front of the frame to dry, then repeat the process on the back.*

Decorating the Mirror Frame

One of the unsung stars of modern technology, the photocopier is a powerful tool for designers. Here repeat patterns are used to bold effect.

Painted paper

MATERIALS
Paper to be patterned
and painted
Color washes
Wallpaper paste
Gouache paint
(gold and copper)
Black wash
Satin polyurethane
varnish

EQUIPMENT
Artist's brush
Paper towels
or sponge
Varnish brush

1 *Make sheets of patterned paper by drawing a design in black and white. Photocopy it enough times to cover the frame. Apply different color washes over the sheets of paper and decorate with squiggles of gold and daubs of color. Tear the sheets into large squares. Dip the patterned pieces of paper in wallpaper paste, then paste onto the drape of the mirror frame, keeping matching colors at the same level on both sides of the drape to give the effect of a real curtain. Then cover the vase with a layer of patterned pieces of paper.*

2 *Paint the shelf of the mirror frame in black paint and leave to dry. Then apply a wash of gold paint over the top and allow to dry again. Daub decorative gold dots onto the vase.*

3 *Using copper gouache paint, paint spots on the vase and add stripes across the drapes and around the edges for a stylish trim. Dip a scrunched-up paper towel or a sponge in copper gouache, dab it on paper to get rid of the excess paint, then dab it all over the shelf to create a textured pattern.*

4 *Using a very diluted black wash, paint shadows in the folds of the drapes and on the vase. The amount you need to use will depend on the brightness of the colors in your decoration. If you have used bright colors, you may need to add more black shading than if you have used pale colors. Let the frame dry.*

5 *Paint the back of the mirror frame with black paint, shading in the edges around the frame. Let dry. Varnish the entire mirror frame for a satin finish, then, when the frame is dry, peel off the plastic sheet protecting the mirror.*

47

Elephant Pot

MATERIALS

Thick cardboard
tube
Thick cardboard
Pencil
Polyvinyl white glue
Newsprint
White latex paint

EQUIPMENT

Scissors
Ruler
Sandpaper
Paintbrush
Craft knife

See p.51 for materials
to decorate the pot.

A HINT OF THE EXOTIC and the warm colors of a Moorish market – yellow ochre, burnt cinnamon, and rich turquoise blue – characterize this container. It possesses a high degree of finesse and uses sophisticated coloring, although the basic technique of building upon an existing cardboard shape simplifies matters. Its surface is evenly tactile, almost like ceramic or gesso, and there is not a bump or a wrinkle in sight – a refinement that requires patient smoothing when applying the paper. Containers using these more subtle colors look good grouped together: a collection of harmonizing pots and jars of different sizes is very handsome.

The decorative motifs on the pot are simple blocked shapes whose outlines can easily be stenciled or traced from an image in a book. Elegant lettering and numerals also take to this finish very well. The technique of building on a cardboard foundation can be adapted to make wider or larger containers, such as Shaker-style boxes or tall painted umbrella stands, using cardboard cylinders of different sizes.

The Lid Fits
This little cylindrical container has the answer to wobbly or loose lids, with its snug liner that holds the top firmly in place. It is easily and quickly made, using existing cardboard tubing, covered with glass-smooth layers of newspaper. Its resulting quiet sophistication is unusual for papier-mâché objects, where theatrical exuberance is more the norm.

Pots of Color
The liveliness of the color comes from the brushed texture of the underlying latex paint and the contrasts between crayon, acrylic paint, and the opaque bands of gold.

Making the Pot

*Sturdy little cylinders to hold kitchen utensils, paintbrushes,
makeup tools and desktop paraphernalia are utter simplicity to
make, using any size of cardboard tube as a foundation.*

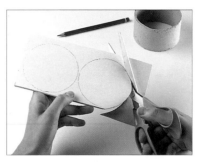

1 *Cut three sections from a cardboard tube, one measuring 3in (7.5cm), one 2½in (6.5cm), and the third 2in (5cm). The largest section will form the base of the pot and the other two pieces will make the lid. Rub the edges of each section with sandpaper to neaten.*

2 *Stand one of the tube sections on a piece of thick cardboard and draw around the base twice. Cut out the two circles. These will form the base and lid of the pot.*

3 *Taking the middle-sized tube section, cut down the length of the tube and trim off a strip approximately ¼in (6mm) wide. Discard the strip and close the cut edges together to give the tube section a smaller circumference. Insert this section inside the smaller tube section, as shown, to make the pot lid.*

4 *Paste polyvinyl glue around one rim of each tube section and glue the two cardboard circles onto these rims to create the base and lid of the pot.*

5 *Tear one large sheet of newsprint into strips approximately 5in (12.5cm) long and 1in (2.5cm) wide. Dip the strips one at a time into diluted polyvinyl glue (3 parts glue to 1 part water) and then paste the paper over the surface of the cardboard pot, smoothing it down with your fingers as you go. Cover the two halves of the pot inside and out, except for the lip of the lid, and leave to dry. Then paste on a second layer of newsprint strips and allow to dry again.*

6 Using a craft knife, score along the edge of the lip of the lid and peel off a thin layer of cardboard all around. The layer should be approximately half the thickness of the cardboard. Smooth down the lip with sandpaper to neaten. This will enable the lid to fit easily into the base of the pot.

7 Apply a coat of white latex paint over the two halves of the pot, both inside and out. Allow to dry and then paint on a second coat. The latex will provide a better surface than cardboard for decorating.

Decorating the Pot
Use different kinds of paint and crayon together to give your pot a vivacious finish.

MATERIALS
Crayons
Acrylic paint
Silver metallic paint
Fixative
Household varnish

EQUIPMENT
Pencil
Paintbrush
Varnish brush

Draw a design in pencil around the outside of the pot. Fill in the pencil outline with a combination of crayon and paint for subtle textural effects. Here the elephants and stars are crayoned, while the background is painted in acrylic paint. Extra decoration is provided by narrow strips of silver metallic paint around the rim and base of the pot. Allow the paint to dry, then spray the pot with fixative, taking care not to inhale any. Apply a coat of varnish.

Kitsch Coffer

MATERIALS

Thin cardboard
Corrugated cardboard
Masking tape
Polyvinyl white glue
Water
Newsprint
Tissue paper
Modeling clay
Petroleum jelly
Quick-acting adhesive
epoxy resin
White
latex paint

EQUIPMENT

Pencil
Scalpel
Metal ruler
Jelly jar
Paintbrush
Cake rack
Spatula

See p.55 for materials
to decorate the coffer.

T HIS CONTAINER is the perfect expression of the irreverent fun to be had with papier-mâché in triumphant tribute to Valentine's Day. Use the coffer to hold wildly expensive chocolates, an amethyst engagement ring on a scarlet velvet pillow, or a collection of ribbon-bound love letters. For a more demure look, you could take seaside colors and attach molded starfish or real shells to the top and sides to make the perfect home for seaside souvenirs.

The box is too glorious to hold anything as banal as seed packets or tax receipts, but a small collection of significant ephemera as an evolving diary to remind you of parties, proposals, and passionate attachments is quite in order. If your courage fails you, it is perfectly permissible to simplify the design. Make your box without feet or double lid, or even molded hearts. You can then build cautiously from your successes, and, if a plain box turns out to be manageable, you might boldly proceed to tackle something more demanding.

A Labor of Love
Built up from a somewhat complex cardboard base, this box has been very carefully designed, despite its look of carefree insouciance. Three-dimensional molded motifs and painstaking paintwork in exuberant colors combine in a container in which to keep your most precious possessions.

Inspired by Fish
The same shape and fishy inspiration with very different results: the black box sets off a kaleidoscope of vibrant clashing color, beside which the shell-studded seaside coffer looks almost quietly naturalistic.

Making the Box

Precise cutting and gluing are essential for the architectural finesse of this coffer, and result in a stunning labor of love, the perfect home for billets-doux.

1 Make six templates (see pp.92–3) from thin cardboard. Draw around the templates on corrugated cardboard and cut out the required number of pieces (you should have 16 in total). For neat edges, use a craft knife held against a metal ruler. Cut the corner edges of the box sides at 45°. This will help the pieces fit together more easily when you assemble the box.

2 Assemble the box and lid following the diagram shown on p.93. Hold the pieces of cardboard in place with strips of masking tape.

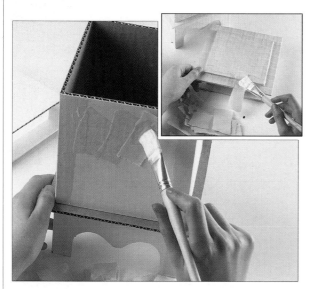

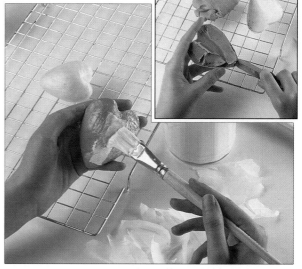

3 Prepare the glue and paper. In a jelly jar, mix 3 parts polyvinyl glue with 1 part water. Tear strips of newsprint and tissue paper about 2 × 1in (5 × 2.5cm). Dipping a brush in the diluted glue mixture, paste a layer of overlapping newsprint strips over all the edges and joints of the box and lid (see inset). Paste both the surface of the box and on top of the paper to make sure it lies flat. Leave to dry for 48 hours.

4 Make two hearts out of modeling clay approximately 2in (5cm) wide and 1in (2.5cm) thick, and a smaller heart approximately 1½ in (4cm) wide and ¾ in (2cm) thick. Cover with petroleum jelly, then, using polyvinyl glue, paste 30 layers of tissue paper over them in the same way as in step 3, p.22. Let the hearts dry on a cake rack for 48 hours, then remove the modeling clay in the same way as in step 4, p.22 (see inset).

5 *Cut out four cardboard heart shapes using the templates (see p.93). Glue one to each side of the box using diluted polyvinyl glue. Glue a papier-mâché heart half onto each cardboard heart; keep two of the larger heart halves for the lid. Then paste three layers of tissue paper over the heart shapes and leave them to dry for 24 hours.*

6 *To make a handle for the lid, cut out an arrow approximately 6in (15cm) long from cardboard (see template on p.93). Paste a layer of tissue paper over the arrow and sandwich it between the two remaining heart halves so that the arrow points downward. Paste six layers of tissue paper over the heart and arrow to secure, and let dry for 24 hours.*

Decorating the Box
Leave your inhibitions behind and enjoy yourself – every fraction of the surface should be alive with vibrant color.

MATERIALS
Gouache paints
Spray varnish
Gloss interior wood varnish

EQUIPMENT
Artist's brush
Varnish brush

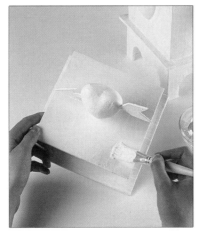

7 *Using a ruler and pencil, draw diagonal lines from corner to corner across the lid of the box to find the center point. Using a spatula, apply epoxy resin adhesive to the base of the heart handle and the center point of the lid and glue the heart handle to the lid. Prop the heart in place for about ten minutes. Paper over the juncture with tissue paper when dry. Let dry for 24 hours.*

8 *Apply a coat of white latex paint over the box and lid, both inside and out, and leave to dry. This will provide a smooth surface for decorating.*

Decorate the box using gouache paints. First apply the base coats, varying them on each side of the box; here the colors used were ochre, red, purple, and violet. Allow to dry, then paint red-brown and black squiggles over the top to create a leopard-skin pattern. Decorate the red and purple areas with gold spots and squiggles. When the paint is dry, apply one thin coat of spray varnish to set the surface of the gouache and allow to dry. Finally paint on two thin coats of gloss interior wood varnish for a tough, shiny surface, allowing the varnish to dry between coats.

Carnival Mask

MATERIALS

Cardboard
Masking tape
Newsprint
Polyvinyl white glue
Water
Modeling clay
Petroleum jelly
Gesso

EQUIPMENT

Pencil
Scissors
Craft knife
Paintbrush
Sandpaper

See p.59 for materials
to decorate the mask.

A MODEL MADE FROM cardboard shaped with modeling clay is used as the mold for this exuberant Mardi Gras mask. The clay face is smoothed over with many layers of newspaper strips to make the refined sculptural curves, and three coats of gesso are used to strengthen the papier-mâché and give a sandable, receptive surface for brilliant work with acrylic paint.

This method offers a wonderful opportunity for custom-made personalized masks for parties, Greek dramas, childrens' theater, or to hang on your walls as slightly sinister trophies of particularly memorable masquerades. This is your chance – exploit it with caution – to indulge in kindly caricature and to give free rein to your decorative whims. Few people will object to being represented as a glorious bird of paradise complete with a tremulous tiara of feathers – but you may lose friends if you portray them in the guise of platypus or pig.

Decorative Disguise
A brilliant piece of bravura painting, this finely detailed feathered mask is too good to waste on a single party, however magnificent, and would make a handsome, if startling, object to hang on your wall. Or it could be just the excuse you need to make a trip to New Orleans at carnival time.

Two Faces of Paper
Acrylic paint is perfect for fine brushwork. These two masks seem to come from an earlier age – the blue bird could grace a renaissance bal masqué, while the sun-bright lion has a strong heraldic flavor.

Making the Mask

Sculpted from modeling clay and cardboard, this fearsome
mask could be adapted to make many different faces – beaks and
snouts are just a matter of altering the cut and shape.

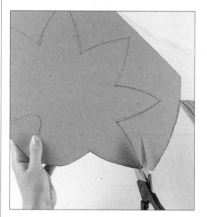

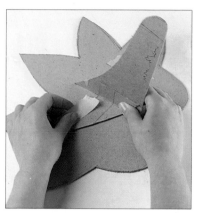

1 *Draw the shape of the mask on cardboard, and then draw the shape of a beak. Cut out both shapes with scissors.*

2 *Position the beak on the mask so that it juts out from the mask at an angle of 90°. Anchor it in place with two pieces of cardboard, taped first to each side of the beak and then to the mask.*

3 *Cover the taped cardboard where the beak joins the mask with torn strips of newsprint, pasted on with a dilute mix of 1 part polyvinyl glue to 1 part water. This will strengthen the joint and make it firm. Let dry for at least a day.*

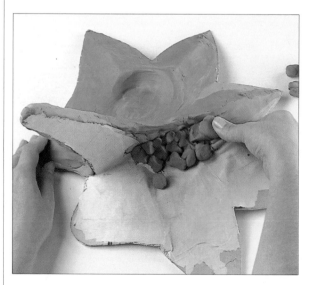

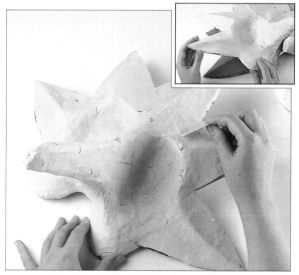

4 *Cover the surface of the mask with small lumps of modeling clay and smooth them down to define the shape of the mask. Build up the features, such as the shape of the beak and hollows for the eyes. Be bold when modeling, because fine details will be painted.*

5 *Cover the clay with petroleum jelly and paste 10 layers of newsprint on the front and back of the mask using diluted glue as before. Let dry for approximately three days, or until the mask is hard and dry. Using a craft knife, cut around the outer edges of the mask and along the length of the beak. Gently peel the mask away from the mold (see inset).*

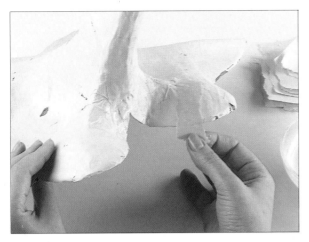

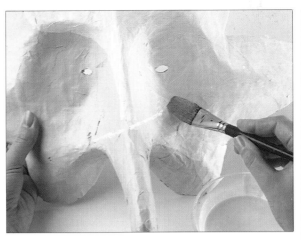

6 *Make eyeholes and holes at the sides of the mask for threading ribbon through. Close the slit in the beak so that it fits snugly, and tape the edges together with masking tape. Then paste strips of newsprint over the joint and around the edges of the mask to smooth any rough areas.*

7 *Paint the mask with three coats of gesso, allowing each coat to dry before applying the next. The gesso will provide a good surface to paint on, and it also strengthens the papier-mâché. When dry, rub the gesso with sandpaper to give it a smooth finish.*

Decorating the Mask

Acrylic paint brings a carnival brightness and intensity of color and allows the finer details of eye and brow to be sharply delineated.

Feathers

MATERIALS
Pale-colored pencil
Acrylic paints
Feathers
Newsprint
Polyvinyl white glue
Interior varnish
Ribbons

EQUIPMENT
Artist's brush
Varnish brush

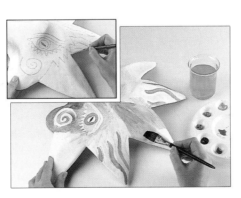

1 *Using a pale-colored pencil, draw the design onto the mask. Do not use an ordinary lead pencil because it might smear when you apply the paint. Apply the acrylic paints, using pale colors first and gradually building up layers of color. Keep the paint fairly watery and, for greater texture, rub the paint into the gesso with your fingers.*

2 *Continue to paint the mask, progressing to darker, stronger colors, such as red and dark green. When you have finished painting the front of the mask, paint the reverse black. Allow the paint to dry, then attach the feathers to the back of the mask at the top with a few strips of pasted newsprint. Allow to dry, then varnish the mask with interior varnish for a glossy finish and protective coat. Finally, thread ribbons through the side holes and use these to tie the mask around your head.*

Ideas to Inspire

By using cardboard, wood, modeling clay, or chicken wire, you can create any shape you want. Included on the following pages are frames, bowls, clocks and dolls, and even a lifelike rooster. Plunder the repertoire to make a Noah's ark or a lamp base, and work your way up to carnival masks and side tables.

▶ **Nursery Dolls**
The heads of these dolls are scrunched-up balls of paper; the limbs and necks are plastic straws, covered with paper, which are attached to the stuffed cotton bodies with thread. Details were painted with acrylic, while the clothes were made from scraps of fabric.

◀ **Spherical Vases**
Molded on a beach ball, these vases were painted with a mixture of latex paint and polyvinyl glue, then painted with acrylics and scumbled with a cloth. Cut-out paper shapes were glued on for additional decoration.

◀ Heraldic Frame
Built from a cardboard framework, this frame was painted with cream and blue acrylic, and rubbed down with sandpaper. The fleurs-de-lis and lettering were treated in the same way.

▶ Love Chest
A battered old chest was layered with colored paper and torn strips of pages from romance novels. When dry, it was painted with latex paint mixed with gouache in shades of pink, light blue, purple, silver, and gold, then rubbed down with sandpaper and varnished.

▲ Shell Clock
Built from recycled cardboard, this clock was covered with mottled handmade paper, then decorated with stenciled shells.

◀ Wreath Frame
This frame was decorated with paper roses and Styrofoam leaves, and given an oil-scumbled glaze.

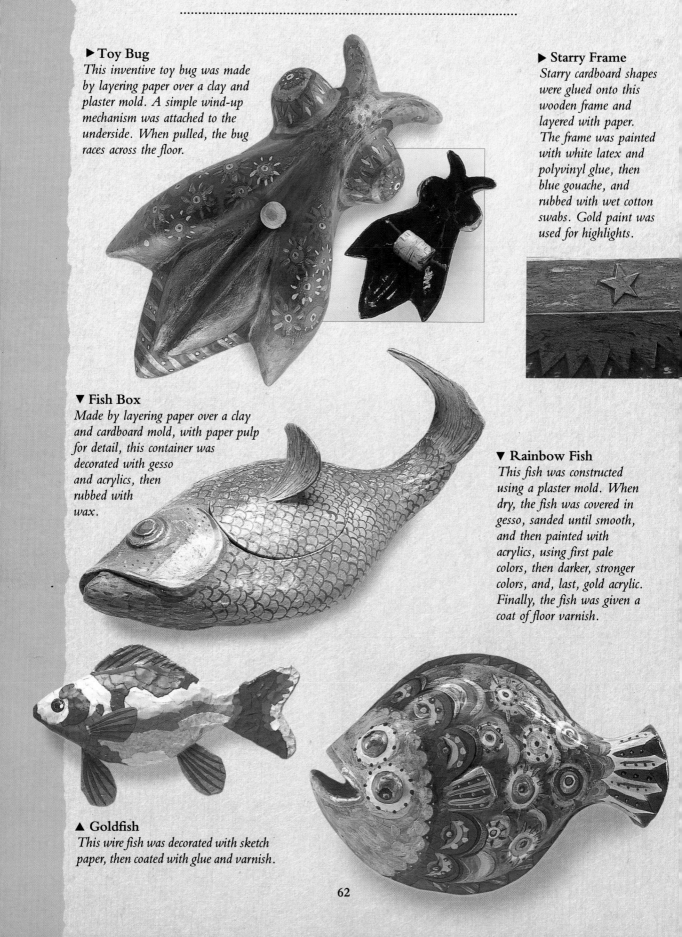

▶ Toy Bug
This inventive toy bug was made by layering paper over a clay and plaster mold. A simple wind-up mechanism was attached to the underside. When pulled, the bug races across the floor.

▶ Starry Frame
Starry cardboard shapes were glued onto this wooden frame and layered with paper. The frame was painted with white latex and polyvinyl glue, then blue gouache, and rubbed with wet cotton swabs. Gold paint was used for highlights.

▼ Fish Box
Made by layering paper over a clay and cardboard mold, with paper pulp for detail, this container was decorated with gesso and acrylics, then rubbed with wax.

▼ Rainbow Fish
This fish was constructed using a plaster mold. When dry, the fish was covered in gesso, sanded until smooth, and then painted with acrylics, using first pale colors, then darker, stronger colors, and, last, gold acrylic. Finally, the fish was given a coat of floor varnish.

▲ Goldfish
This wire fish was decorated with sketch paper, then coated with glue and varnish.

◄ Paper Poultry

A wire mesh structure was used as a base for this rooster. The shape was built up with layers of paper coated with wallpaper paste. When dry, the rooster was painted with acrylics and finally varnished. The effect is so lifelike that some of the artist's real hens have had to look twice!

▼ Giant Fish Plaque

Measuring 37in (93cm) long and 20in (50cm) wide, this plaque was constructed by layering newsprint in a plaster mold. When dry, the mold was pried off and the fish given four coats of gesso, sanded until smooth, and then decorated with acrylics and varnished.

Decorative Ideas and Finishes

·······································

YOU'VE COME TO GRIPS with the preliminaries, and can now indulge in the fine art of fancy decoration. This is where your imagination can run wild; you can cover your papier-mâché with gesso for a porcelain-smooth finish; discover the splendor conferred by metal and gold leaf, or the satisfying antiquity that crackle glaze emulates; experiment with stitching and embossing, or decorate with glitter or glass jewels. Be bold and sassy with outrageous color, or use more natural colors with shells and colored glass as ornamentation.

Remember that no matter how many old newspapers you recycle this way, next Sunday will bring a fresh deluge to contend with.

Butterfly Tray

MATERIALS

Hardboard,
⅛in (2mm) thick,
or mat board
Cardboard
Polyvinyl white glue
Masking tape
Cellulose wallpaper
paste
Newsprint

EQUIPMENT

Scissors
Wooden match or
toothpick
Paintbrush

See p.68 for materials
to decorate the tray.

THE JAPANESE do not have a monopoly on tea. With a bit of effort and a dash of style, you can create your own tea ceremony in recollection of better and more civilized times. Fine translucent china cups, a flowery teapot, buttered muffins, and a bouquet of butterflies on an artfully painted and aged tray will bring a touch of summer to fireside feasts.

This is your chance to exploit the pleasures of decoupage, or the inspired use of the color photocopier. A large flat surface is an invitation to have fun; with practice you will soon produce something pretty and personal. Try painting a freehand trompe-l'oeil of cookies and cakes, decoupage a potted primrose from gift wrap, try your hand at calligraphy to make an inscribed anniversary present, or stencil a chrysanthemum and splatter it in gold. You have the world on a tray.

Picnic Tea
Never mind the weather – a tray of butterflies will bring a scent of high summer, buddleias, and blossoms to the most withering winter. Decoupage is fun and easy to do, and begs to be used as a lasting reminder of past pleasures: a wedding can be celebrated with valentine hearts and cherubs, while a sunny summer vacation can be remembered with shells and tropical fish.

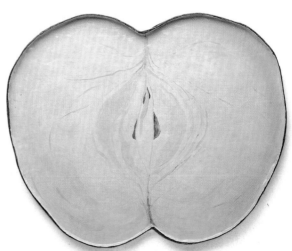

Autumn Harvest
Once smitten, you will find all sorts of unexpected things make terrific color photocopies: fiery fall leaves, with possibly a pheasant's feather and a fern frond, will summon the season of fog and wood smoke; or take your inspiration from autumn apples for a "fruitful" tray.

Making the Tray

Papier-mâché can be combined with anything. Here,
hardboard is given a thin veneer of paper for character.

1 Cut a circle, about 12in (30cm) in diameter, from thick hardboard or mat board. Cut a strip of cardboard, approximately ⅝ in (1.5cm) wide and long enough to go around the edge of the circle. You may find it easier to cut two strips and then attach them separately. Using a match or toothpick, apply polyvinyl glue around the edge of the hardboard circle.

2 Attach the strip of cardboard to the edge of the hardboard circle to make the rim of the tray (the smooth side of the hardboard should be facing upward). Hold the strips in place with masking tape as you go. Join the two edges of the cardboard neatly when you complete the circle. Paint the underside of the tray with a coat of polyvinyl glue to seal and waterproof it. Let the tray to dry thoroughly.

3 Using cellulose wallpaper paste, paste thin strips of newsprint over the rim of the tray, wrapping them from the inside to the outside of the rim and pressing them down firmly into the joint. Paste larger strips of newsprint over the base of the tray until the whole tray is covered. Repeat to cover the tray with a second layer, and leave the tray to dry. Apply two more layers of paper and allow to dry.

Decorating the Tray

All you need for decoupage is a spirit of ruthless
plagiarism, a good pair of scissors, and some glue.

MATERIALS
Gesso tinted
with pigment
Acrylic paint
Paper motifs
cut from magazines
Paper glue
Acrylic high-build
decoupage varnish
Dark-colored
wax polish

EQUIPMENT
Medium-grade
sandpaper
Housepainter's brush
Medium- and coarse-
grade steel wool
Scissors
Paper towels
Artist's brush
Varnish brush
Cloth

1 Lightly sand all surfaces of the tray to remove any uneven bumps. Then apply three layers of gesso tinted with pigment, allowing the tray to dry between coats. Lightly sand the tray before applying the last coat.

2 Paint random patches of three or four colors of acrylic paint over the surface of the tray – here white, yellow, green, and burgundy. Mix and merge the colors together for a subtle summery effect and allow the tray to dry thoroughly.

3 *Gently rub the tray with sandpaper to allow some of the gesso base to show through the paint. Then rub medium-grade steel wool over the surface.*

4 *Place the paper motifs upside down on a paper towel, brush with paper glue (see inset), then place them glue side down on the surface of the tray in a design of your choosing. Using a scrunched-up paper towel, blot the glued paper motifs thoroughly to absorb any excess glue and to remove any air bubbles. Any fine details can be painted onto the tray at this stage. Allow to dry.*

5 *Apply a minimum of six layers of varnish to the tray, allowing each layer to dry before applying the next. The rim and underside of the tray should have an extra three layers of varnish for protection. When the varnish is dry, rub coarse-grade steel wool over the surface of the tray in a circular motion. This will remove some of the shine and cover the surface with random scratches.*

6 *Using a soft cloth, rub dark-colored fine wax polish into the scratch marks on the surface of the tray. Allow the polish to dry for approximately 45 minutes, then rub off with a clean cloth. The dark-colored polish will remain in the cracks to give the tray an aged and worn appearance*

Opulent Earrings

MATERIALS

Thick cardboard
Quick-acting epoxy
resin adhesive
Earring findings
Newsprint
Wallpaper paste
White latex paint

EQUIPMENT

Pencil
Scissors
Toothpick
Bowl
Cake rack
Paintbrush
Pliers

See p.73 for materials
to decorate the
earrings.

THESE EARRINGS deliver a high dose of drama but, unlike the Koh-i-noor diamond, they need not hide in the safe when they are not adorning your ears. They are a glorious example of the wit and inventiveness that modern jewelry designers are bringing to their craft. They are also cheeringly simple to make, inviting experiment and variation.

The creator of these earrings also makes magnificent bangles and brooches, building on a basic shape of twisted paper for the former and using a cardboard foundation for the latter. Having succeeded with the earrings, you could turn your hand to sets of coordinated theatrical jewelry to match particular outfits. Try personalizing a pair of earrings to make an unforgettable birthday present for a friend. Or celebrate special occasions with custom-made creations. Christmas, for example, might bring you out in the classic color combinations of red, green, and gold; scarlet and magenta hearts could be just the thing for Valentine's Day; or a favorite brocade jacket might suggest earrings and a brooch that pick up its colors and motifs. Above all, this kind of jewelry is great fun to make and should be worn in the same spirit.

Thrifty Glitter
Projecting a quite disproportionate degree of glamour, thanks to their witty, glittery finish, these earrings are easy to make. They do not pretend to be anything precious, just a bright kaleidoscope of gold paint, foil, and fake gemstones.

Hearts and Stars
How to get dazzling mileage out of paint and paper clips – dangling Mexican-bright hearts are made from nothing more exotic than paper, paint, and glue, while the spotted stars benefit from an ingenious halo of paper clips.

Making the Earrings

Hearts for Valentine's Day, stars for Christmas, diamonds if you can't afford the real thing – these earrings can be any shape you like and, thanks to their lightness, any size, too.

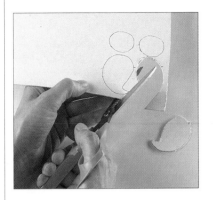 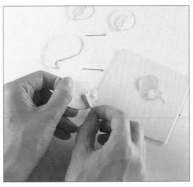 

1 *Draw the shape of your earrings on thick cardboard. Each of these earrings has two sections, a small circular shape for the top of the earring, and a comma shape that will hang from this. Cut out the shapes with scissors.*

2 *Using a toothpick, apply epoxy resin adhesive to each earring shape and glue an earring finding on each so that the loop of the finding overlaps the edge in each case. These findings will be used to hook the top and bottom shapes together. Let them dry for one to two hours.*

3 *Tear two layers of newsprint into strips 2in (5cm) long and 1in (2.5cm) wide. Mix up a small amount of wallpaper paste according to the manufacturer's instructions. Dip one strip at a time into the paste, then paste it over the cardboard shapes and smooth it down. Cover both sides of each shape, then leave them on a cake rack to dry overnight. Repeat the whole process.*

 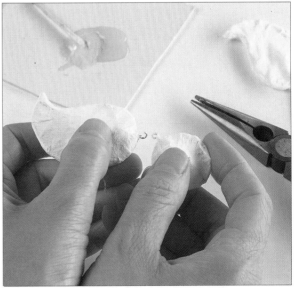

4 *Having checked they are dry, paint the earring shapes on both sides with a coat of white latex paint and let dry. The paint will provide a better surface than newsprint for decorating the earrings.*

5 *To attach the earring sections together, pry open the ring on the bottom section of the finding with pliers and hook this through the loop on the top section. Bend back the hook to close it, and set it with epoxy resin adhesive.*

Decorating the Earrings

Paint, candy wrappers, and gemstones make these showstoppers. You could experiment with gold leaf for substance, or holiday glitter for seasonal style.

Flat-backed gemstones

Colored foil

MATERIALS
Gouache paints
Rapid epoxy resin
Flat-backed
   gemstones
   *(available from
   craft stores)*
Colored foil
Clear gloss
   polyurethane
   varnish

EQUIPMENT
Artist's brush
Toothpick
Scissors
Newspaper

1 *Using gouache paints, paint different-colored stripes on both sides of the earrings to cover the white latex completely. This will provide the background color for the earrings. Let dry.*

2 *Applying epoxy resin adhesive with a toothpick, glue several flat-backed gemstones onto the front of each earring. Use a variety of different colors and sizes of gemstones for a dazzling effect. Let dry.*

3 *Cut strips of colored foil about ¼ in (6mm) wide. Using a toothpick, apply epoxy resin adhesive around one gemstone at a time. Position a strip of foil on the glued area around the gemstone, pushing it into place carefully with your fingers as you go. Cut off any spare foil. Repeat the process for each gemstone.*

4 *For extra sparkle, paint the edges of each earring with gold gouache paint. Let dry for approximately half an hour.*

5 *Using epoxy resin adhesive, glue an earring finding to the back of each earring. Leave to dry until the findings are firmly set.*

6 *Holding the earrings by their back findings, dip them into a can of clear gloss polyurethane varnish to coat them completely. Lay them on newspaper and leave to dry. The varnish gives the earrings extra shine and a protective coat.*

Precious Paper

MATERIALS
Toilet paper
Water
Casein paint or gesso

EQUIPMENT
Metal skewers or
knitting needles
Bowl
Jelly jar
Cake pan (optional)
Artist's brush

See p.76 for materials
to decorate the beads.

SUBTLE GLINTS OF COLOR and gold, as smoothly faceted as the opalescent interior of an oyster's shell – these lustrous trinkets are child's play to make, and they look sumptuous in generous swags as the sole and sophisticated adornment of a simple black dress. The technique could not be easier, and the resulting beads can be ornate or plain, smooth or textured, shiny or matte, slender tubes, or dumpy spheres.

You could paint them with loose dashes of color, as here, or with fine detail using acrylic or gouache and a small sable brush. Try painting dots, stripes, or zigzags in bright rainbows, or in one or two colors to match an outfit. You could stipple your beads like a quail's egg, or emboss them with a toothpick and give them the aged look of verdigris with green and turquoise. Thread your beads on fine, shiny silk cord, a colored leather thong knotted between each bead, or a natural string to link beads of black, cinnabar, and gold.

Sumptuous Baubles
If you are of the school of thought that believes big is best, and lots is even better when it comes to finery, then a king's ransom of papier-mâché baubles is for you.

Spangle Power
Raid the rainbow, add silver and gold, and you have an unbeatable recipe for visual riches. Who needs diamonds when all the color in the world is at the tip of your paintbrush?

Making the Beads

So simple a child could do it, and so effective that an adult might just take a try – beads of all sizes and shapes are the work of a moment.

1 *Wrap a length of toilet paper around a skewer or knitting needle several times, and then dip it into a bowl of water and squeeze out as much as possible, shaping the bead as you go. Push the bead down the skewer and repeat the process with another length of paper. When you have four beads on the skewer, place the skewer in a jelly jar and let the beads dry. Alternatively, speed up the drying time considerably by slipping the beads off the skewer and putting them in a cake pan in an oven at a very low setting. Check them every ten minutes or so.*

2 *Mix casein paint to the consistency of heavy cream. Paint this onto the beads to cover them completely and let dry. The casein paint will provide a smooth surface to paint on. You could also paint the beads with gesso for a similar finish.*

Decorating the Beads

A chance to run wild with color and gold leaf – get inspiration from textiles or embroidery.

Silver leaf   Gold leaf

MATERIALS
Opaque, pearlescent
and transparent acrylic inks
Transparent watercolor ink
Gold and silver poster paints
High-gloss clear polyurethane varnish
Silver and gold leaf
Decorative cord or leather thong

EQUIPMENT
Artist's brush
Varnish brush

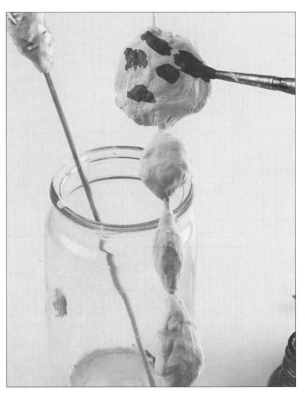

1 *Using colored acrylic inks – opaque, pearlescent, and transparent – daub dots of color onto the beads.*

2 *Gradually cover the entire surface of the beads with dots and strokes of color, building up the effect using opaque, then pearlescent, and then transparent ink, overlaying different colors. Allow the beads to dry.*

3 *Next paint the beads with sepia transparent watercolor ink to tone down the bright colors of the acrylic ink and create an antiquing effect. Let the beads dry for a few minutes.*

4 *Smudge gold and silver poster paint on the beads with a semidry brush, allowing the base colors to show through. Let the beads dry, then apply two to five coats of polyurethane gloss varnish, allowing each coat to dry before applying the next.*

5 *Press small torn pieces of silver and gold leaf onto the beads, pressing and smoothing out with the ball of the thumb. Finally apply another coat of varnish for a high-gloss finish and allow to dry. To make the beads into a necklace, twist them off the skewer, carefully smoothing away any rough edges where the hole passes through the bead, and thread them onto a length of cord or a leather thong.*

Copper-Stemmed Vase

MATERIALS

Medium-weight
cardboard
Masking tape
Flour
Water
Newsprint

EQUIPMENT

Metal ruler
Scissors
Protractor
Pencil
String

See p.80 for materials
to decorate the vase.

A VASE THAT FLOATS on its own copper curlicue, an elegant tapered cone vibrant with the partnership of indigo outside and a gleaming metallic throat within, would make the perfect receptacle for a swath of peacocks' feathers or fronds of airy dried flowers. But the more ambitious or adventurous – with ready access to a soldering iron – can make a glittering bouquet of brass stars and hearts, leaves and teardrops, attached to copper wire, which will shiver and twinkle with every breath of wind.

This vase, whose uneven shadowed and shining surface shows off the inimitable richness of metal leaf, uses a simply constructed foundation of cardboard, while loose pigment gives it velvety depth of color. The result is a beautiful object, delicate and elegant, like an upturned flower. A pair of them would make a graceful addition to a mantelpiece, while different sizes in harmonizing shades of one color would make a handsome group.

Velvet Color
Elegance in triplicate, the use of loose powder pigment gives an astonishing matte richness of color to these vases, in contrast to the swirl of a copper stem and the gleaming metal leaf.

Precious Metal Bowl
Nothing beats metal leaf for a glamorous transformation. Applying it is a little awkward but not difficult, and you will soon be hooked and find yourself looking around for objects to gild. Gold, silver, and copper look decadently opulent together.

Making the Vase

The smooth and elegant line of this vase is easy to achieve. As you become more proficient, you can experiment with different basic shapes.

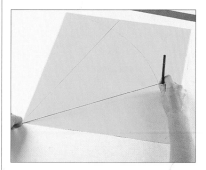

1 *Cut a piece of cardboard 16½in (42cm) square. To make the curved shape, measure 25° at the top left corner of the cardboard using a protractor and mark with a pencil. Tie a piece of string onto the end of the pencil. With one hand, hold the pencil upright on the mark in the top left corner. With the other hand, pull the string taut and hold the end over the bottom left corner. Draw a curved edge from the top left corner to the bottom right corner of the cardboard.*

2 *Cut along the curved edge. Roll the cardboard between your hands to make a cone shape. The cardboard will have a double thickness. Stick strips of masking tape along the edge to keep the cone shape. Finally, secure even more by sticking a piece of tape down the entire length of the joint.*

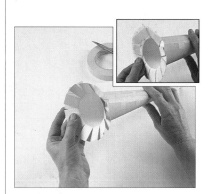

3 *Using scissors, make cuts about 1¼in (3cm) long into the top of the cone, taking each layer of cardboard individually. Leave gaps of ⅝in (1.5cm) between cuts. Fold the cut ends down to form the rim of the vase. Place small strips of masking tape around the top and underside of the rim to strengthen it and make it even (see inset).*

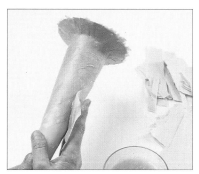

4 *Make up the paste by whisking 1 tablespoon of flour and 1¼ cups (10 fl oz/315ml) water over gentle heat until the mixture begins to boil. Allow to cool. Paste small strips of newsprint inside the vase to a depth of 3in (7.5cm). Then cover the outside with a layer of overlapping paper strips, and finally paste two layers over the rim. Leave the edges around the rim rough. Let dry overnight.*

Decorating the Vase

MATERIALS
Gesso
Pink acrylic paint
Cobalt blue powdered pigment
Fixative
Purple soft artist's pastel
Red oxide metal primer
Gold size
Copper leaf
Metallic bronze powder
62in (1.5m) copper microbore tubing,
¼in (5mm) thick
Brass sheeting
Thin copper wire

EQUIPMENT
Paintbrush
Cotton balls
Scissors
Fork
Soldering iron

1 *Apply two coats of gesso, both inside and outside the vase, to stiffen the cardboard and give a textured surface. When dry, apply a coat of pink acrylic paint to the outside and let dry.*

2 *Using cotton balls, dab blue powdered pigment over the entire surface of the vase. Rub it for an interesting effect. Spray the vase with fixative to set the pigment in place, taking care not to inhale any. This will dry almost immediately.*

3 *Rub a purple soft artist's pastel over the rim of the vase and smear it with your fingers to create patches of intense color. Spray with fixative to set the pastel.*

4 *Paint the inside of the vase with red oxide metal primer and allow to dry thoroughly. Apply a thin, even coat of gold size to the inside and the rim and leave for approximately 30 minutes until it squeaks when rubbed with a finger. Lay pieces of copper leaf onto the size, blowing on it to make it lie flat if necessary, then smooth it down with your fingers. Afterward, rub off any excess with your fingers.*

5 *Dip a cotton ball into metallic bronze powder, then tap the cotton ball over the vase so that the dust drops inside the vase to coat the size. (Be careful to protect your surfaces because metallic powder gets everywhere.) Continue the process until the size is covered with bronze dust. Then spray fixative inside the vase to set the metallic powder in place.*

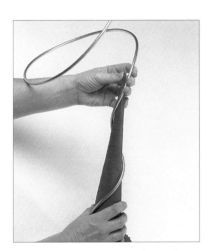

6 *Take the copper microbore tubing, and, holding the top of it tightly in one hand, coil it around the vase twice. Then coil the other end of the tubing to make a flat base for the vase so that it stands upright.*

7 *To make copper stems, cut out decorative shapes, such as circles, hearts, leaves, teardrops, and stars, from a sheet of brass. Press down hard with the end of a fork into the surface of each brass shape to make patterned indentations.*

8 *Take a strip of thin copper wire 28in (70cm) long. Lay it on a brass shape and solder the two together using a hot soldering iron (follow the manufacturer's instructions). Repeat until you have several copper stems with a brass shape at the end of each. These stems can be inserted in the vase.*

Bole Bowl

MATERIALS

Plastic wrap
Newsprint
Rabbit-skin glue
Water
Rabbit-skin gesso

EQUIPMENT

Bowl for mold
Double boiler
Paintbrush
Silicon carbide
sandpaper

See p.84 for materials
to decorate the bowl.
Bole is available
by mail order
from International
Gilder's Supplies
(613) 744-4282.

THIS MAGNIFICENT BOWL is a virtuoso exercise in skill and patience, using traditional methods and materials to achieve a finish of professional marble-smoothness. The artist who made this huge container, which measures 15¼in (38cm) in diameter, demonstrates a fluent expertise that is the result of much experience. The finished object is not too difficult to make, although it requires a little uninterrupted dedication.

Its cool tactile perfection is owed to multiple coats of rabbit-skin gesso applied to a simple layered base. The final result is heavier and more substantial than plain papier-mâché, and the gesso completely obliterates the bowl's humble newspaper origins. Subtle shades of Wedgwood blue and slate brown pigment were applied using a fine clay, known as bole, adding another layer to the refinement of the surface texture. Finally, this sophisticated piece was given a touch of water gilding, whose initial harsh glare was muted with a magical trick of alchemy relying on nothing more mysterious than a hard-boiled egg. This is a piece to work up to, and one of which you can feel jubilantly proud.

Black Beauty

This is a bowl that invites a caress – all that patient work with layers of gesso gives a seductive solidity and elegant smoothness to the finish. The combination of polished bole and antiqued silver is about as grand as paper can aspire to.

Gesso Finesse

Humble beginnings transformed in a small miracle of skill – vary color and motif as you will; paper and gesso combined with finesse result in pure sophistication.

Making the Bowl

*Probably the most demanding project in the book, this
bowl is not quick to make and requires a certain perfectionism
in the finish, but the result is in a league of its own.*

1 *Cover a mold with plastic wrap
Then paste about 10 layers of
long paper strips over the plastic wrap,
from top to bottom, using rabbit-skin
glue. To prepare the glue, mix 1 part
rabbit-skin glue with 10 parts water.
Gently heat in a double boiler until
the glue is hot. Let the bowl dry, then
remove from the mold.*

2 *Paint rabbit-skin gesso onto the
outside of the paper bowl and
then the inside and let dry. Repeat
until you have applied between 10
and 20 layers – the more layers of
gesso you paint on, the better the
finish will be. Allow each coat to dry
before applying the next one.*

3 *Using silicon carbide sandpaper,
sand the surface of the bowl to
remove any bumps and unevenness,
until it feels as smooth as porcelain.*

Decorating the Bowl

*The dark luster of bole makes a magnificent foil for the
interesting alchemy of ancient silver conjured with an egg.*

MATERIALS
Blue bole (*see p.82*)
Rabbit-skin glue
Blue-brown bole mix
Brown bole
Tracing paper
Low-tack tape
Water mixed with
rubbing alcohol
Silver leaf
Hard-boiled egg
Superfine white shellac

EQUIPMENT
Nylon pantyhose
Soft paintbrush
Fine-grade steel wool
Scissors
Pencil
Squirrel-hair brush
Gilder's tip
Cotton balls
Agate burnisher

1 *Prepare the bole (a fine clay) by mixing
1 heaped teaspoon with a little rabbit-
skin glue (which should be no warmer than
room temperature) until the mixture is the
thickness of cream. Strain through nylon
pantyhose. Using a soft brush, apply three
coats of blue bole mix onto the bowl, brushing
quickly. Then apply one or two coats of blue-
brown bole and finally a coat of brown bole.*

2 *When the bowl has dried, take a pad of
fine-grade steel wool and rub it over the
surface of the bowl to give it a soft sheen.*

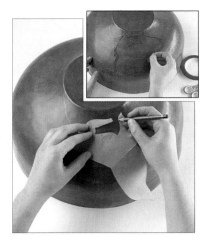

3 *Cut out decorative shapes from tracing paper – here, different animals – and draw around the shape on the outside of the bowl using a pencil. These shapes will then be gilded on the bowl. Stick small pieces of low-tack tape around the edge of the drawn shape on the bowl to mask off the edge of the area to be gilded (see inset).*

4 *Using a squirrel-hair brush, brush water mixed with a drop of rubbing alcohol over the surface of the shape to be gilded, keeping within the masked area. The water will bring the rabbit-skin glue in the gesso to the surface of the bowl, enabling the silver leaf to adhere.*

5 *Working quickly and using a gilder's tip, lay a piece of silver leaf carefully on the wet surface of the bowl. Tap it into position with a soft brush. Repeat to cover all the area to be gilded, then let dry.*

6 *Rub the surface of the silver leaf with a cotton ball to smooth it down and rub off any overlapping pieces. Carefully remove the low-tack tape from around the edges and the gilded shape will be revealed.*

7 *Burnish the gilded areas with an agate burnisher. This presses the silver leaf down securely, smooths out any creases, and brings out the shine. For extra decorative effect, place the bowl upside down over a chopped, newly hard-boiled egg. The sulfur from the egg will tarnish and mottle the silver leaf. Seal the bowl with superfine white shellac, applied with a soft brush. Rub the surface with fine-grade steel wool, then apply a final layer of shellac.*

Festive Star Bowl

MATERIALS

Balloon
Cardboard
String
Newsprint
Polyvinyl white glue
Water
Gold mirrored paper
Red acetate
Parchment paper
Water-based gloss
varnish

EQUIPMENT

Plate
Scissors
Craft knife
Flowerpot
Housepainter's brush
Pencil
Varnish brush

THE TECHNIQUE OF INSERTING colored acetate in rich stained-glass colors into papier-mâché is an original one, and would lend itself (with all due precautions) to making lanterns from which a night-light could twinkle. Put one on a windowsill to welcome winter visitors, or in summer you could hang one from a tree to bring star-spangled enchantment to your garden. Or you could simply use it as a decoration, piled high with Christmas baubles.

The red stars could be replaced by simple geometric cut-outs in rainbow colors for a child's room, or narrow strips of brilliant blue in a black-and-silver ground for a more sophisticated look. The combination of opaque and transparent color begs to be shown off in changing lights: placed on a sunny windowsill, the bowls cast stars upon the paintwork; by candlelight, they have a mysterious glow.

Christmas Stars
The white and gold of this bowl are decidedly celebratory colors, while the sprinkling of transparent scarlet stars adds to the feeling of Christmas. Make a bunch of them to grace a winter windowsill.

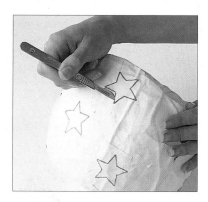

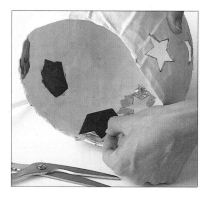

1 *Make a layered bowl using a balloon as a mold (see p.30) Rip the top edge all around to create an undulating rim. Make a star template from cardboard and draw around this all over the outside of the paper bowl. Then, using a craft knife, cut out the star shapes from the outside.*

2 *Bind the cut edges with small strips of gold mirrored paper or foil, wrapping the paper from the outside to the inside of the bowl. Add a small strip across each point of the star on the outside of the bowl, so that each star is completely surrounded with gold.*

3 *Using polyvinyl glue, paste pieces of red acetate over the inside of each cut-out star. Hold the acetate in position with a weight while it dries. Then paste torn strips of parchment paper on the outside of the bowl, leaving a narrow gold edging around each star, and small strips of gold mirrored paper on the inside. Paint the bowl with diluted polyvinyl glue to seal the surface, then varnish it with water-based gloss varnish.*

Ideas to Inspire

With the basics of making and molding under your belt, let your creative side take over and go wild with paint, powders, threads, and jewels, or anything else you desire. Keep your eyes open and you will find a use for feathers and glitter, shiny cord and patterned shells, copper wire and pieces of frosted glass.

▶ **Stitched Up**
Constructed from paper pulp, this bowl was decorated with stitched fabric and paper, and string arches covered with gold tissue paper, then rubbed with shoe polish for an aged effect.

▶ **Calligraphy Bowl**
Created by a calligrapher who uses papier-mâché as a vehicle for her lettering, this bowl has a smooth finish, made by layering over a glass mold and sanding with an electric sander.

◀ **Medieval Coffer**
Medieval church ornamentation was the inspiration for this coffer, which was made from cardboard decorated with string, cardboard shapes, and beads. It was painted with latex and poster paints, then varnished and sponged with gold acrylic.

▲ Zebra Clock
Constructed simply from a cardboard frame and layers of paper, this clock would add a touch of humor to any mantelpiece. It was painted with acrylics and latex paint, and Japanese papers were glued on for contrast. The zebra was modeled from pulp and glued on.

◄ Pedestal Bowl
The pedestal of this bowl was formed by rolling up strips of glue-covered newsprint into a tube shape and, when dry, pasting this to the bowl. The bowl was painted with acrylics, sponged with gold gouache paint, and decorated with collage before being varnished.

▲ Statuesque Cabinet
Measuring 6ft (1.8m) tall, this impressive cabinet was constructed from pulp applied over a plywood framework. Wavy lines, dots, triangles, and swirls of pulp were added for relief decoration. The cabinet was sponged with acrylic paint and decorated with colored foil, while the relief decoration was gilded.

◄ Painted Tissue Clock
This clock was created by
first decorating tissue paper
with dry pigment colors,
metallic powders, acrylics
and oil paints.
When dry, layers of
painted tissue were
applied onto a piece
of hardboard cut into
the desired shape.
Inserting the clock
mechanism is a
straightforward
process.

▼ Spiky Frame
The surface of this unusually shaped
frame, made from a cardboard base
covered with newsprint, was
decorated with paint, colored tissue,
sketch paper and construction paper.
Pieces of broken mirror were glued
onto the frame and highlights were
picked out in gold leaf.

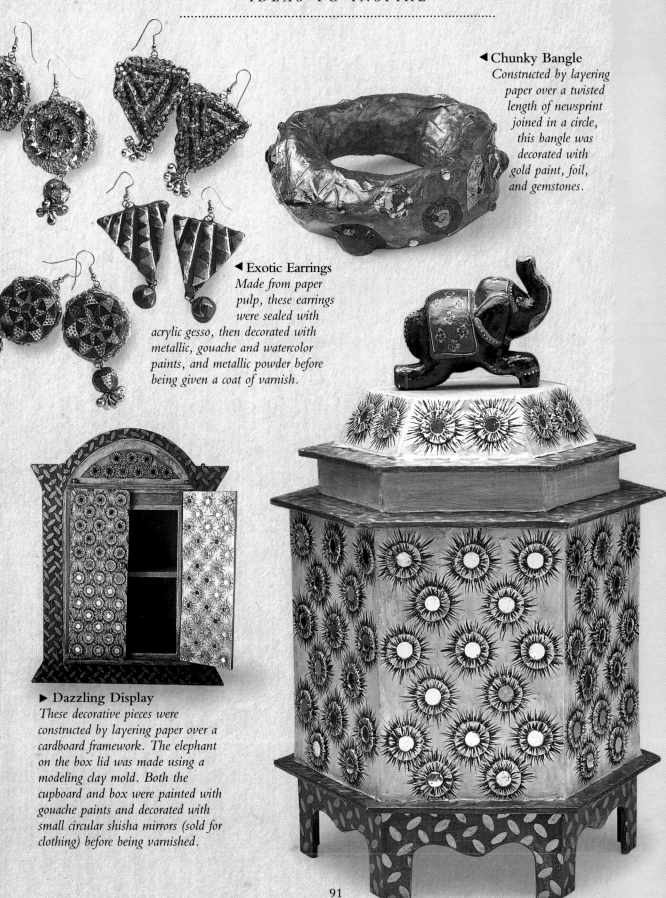

◄ **Chunky Bangle**
Constructed by layering paper over a twisted length of newsprint joined in a circle, this bangle was decorated with gold paint, foil, and gemstones.

◄ **Exotic Earrings**
Made from paper pulp, these earrings were sealed with acrylic gesso, then decorated with metallic, gouache and watercolor paints, and metallic powder before being given a coat of varnish.

▶ Dazzling Display
These decorative pieces were constructed by layering paper over a cardboard framework. The elephant on the box lid was made using a modeling clay mold. Both the cupboard and box were painted with gouache paints and decorated with small circular shisha mirrors (sold for clothing) before being varnished.

Templates

Shown here are the templates for two of the projects featured earlier in the book. Enlarge the templates to the required size on a photocopier, keeping all the templates from one project in proportion to one another.

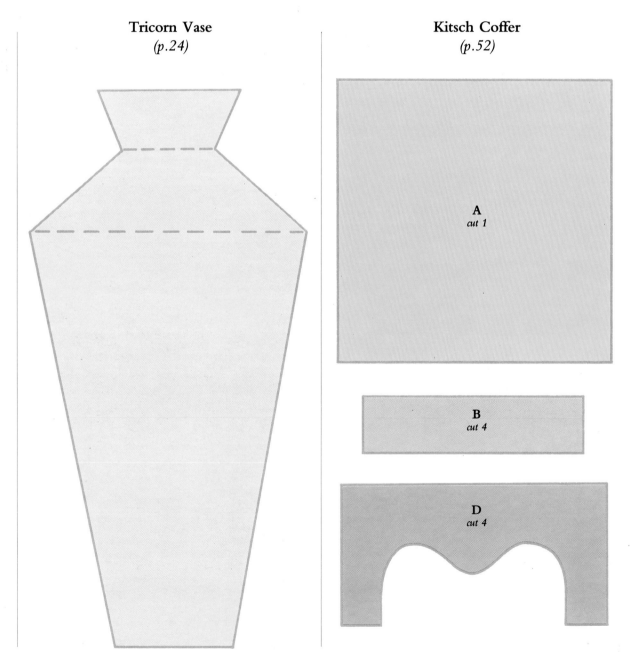

Tricorn Vase
(p.24)

Kitsch Coffer
(p.52)

A
cut 1

B
cut 4

D
cut 4

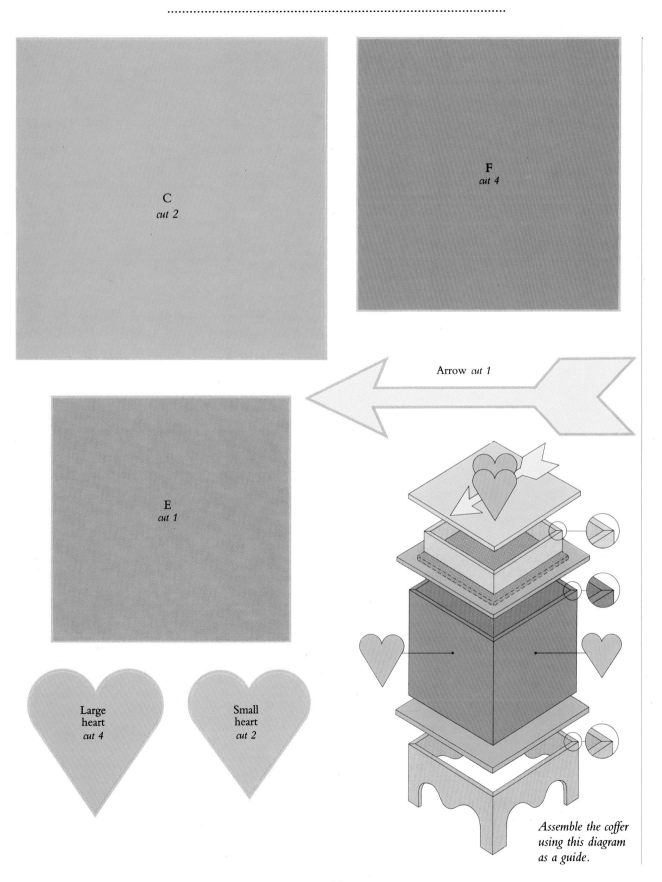

C
cut 2

F
cut 4

Arrow *cut 1*

E
cut 1

Large
heart
cut 4

Small
heart
cut 2

*Assemble the coffer
using this diagram
as a guide.*

Contributors

Madeleine Adams,
*Urn (pp.32-33); bowls
(p.35 top); lidded box
(pp.48-51).*

Julie Arkell,
*Earrings (pp.70-73);
bangle (p.91).*

Rhoda Baker,
Frame (p.61 top).

Hilary Bravo,
*Bowl (pp.28-31);
beads (pp.74-77)*

Patrick Burton,
Clock (p.90).

Ann Carter,
*Fish box (p.62 centre);
tray (pp.66-69).*

**Tim Chesters/Diana
Longenberg
(Chameleons),**
Clock (p.61).

Gerry Copp,
Clock (pp.40-43).

Hazel Dolby,
Bowl (p.88 centre).

Hannah Downes,
Frame (p.63).

Margaret Frere-Smith,
Cockerel (p.63).

Ann Frith,
Cupboard (p.89).

Martin Hall,
Vase (pp.24-27).

Carol Hill,
*Bowl (pp.12-15); bowl
(pp.16-19); bowls
(p.36 bottom).*

Kim & Di Hincks,
*Dish (pp.20-23); casket
(pp.52-55); wall cupboard
(p.91); box (p.91).*

Kim Homer,
Bowls (p.37).

Julie Howells,
*Bowls (p.36);
earrings (p.91).*

Sarah Kelly,
*Plate (p.35 bottom);
goldfish (p.62 bottom right);
bowl (pp.86-87).*

Alice Leach,
Bowl (pp.82-85).

Rosemary Mackinder,
Bowl (p.88 top).

Joanne McCrum,
*Bowls (p.34 and p.35
bottom left); vases (p.60).*

Julie Mosley,
Chest (p.61).

Jennie Neame,
*Curtained mirror
(pp.44-47).*

Glynis Porter,
Clock (p.89).

Carolyn Sansbury,
*Bowl (p.2); vase
(pp.78-81).*

Eleanor Staley,
Casket (p.88).

Yanina Temple,
Bowl (p.89); frame (p.90).

Jan Tricker,
Frame (p.61 bottom).

**John Tutton/Sarah
Young (Odyssey),**
*Mask (p.56); toy bug
(p.62); fish plaques
(p.62 bottom right
and p.63).*

Melanie Williams,
Dolls (p.60).

Index

Acknowledgments

This book owes its inspiration to a thrilling crescendo of work which has recently brought a new vitality to craft exhibitions. The makers who participated in this book were extraordinarily generous – with their time and their ideas – which is typical of their tribe, and makes them such a rare and precious breed. People who make things are just much nicer than the rest of us! I am very grateful to everyone who contributed work; each piece is special in some way, and the torrent of jokey, whimsical and appealing creativity is wonderfully cheering in a world ruled by the strictures of profit and loss. Many thanks to Circus Arts in Brighton who were inspiring and generous with loaning pieces for the book, also to Stuart Stevenson who lent a wide range of paints and papers. The Herculean labour of organizing and editing this book was the lot of Heather Dewhurst, who performed it with exemplary efficiency and calm. Steven Wooster transformed the raw material to make the elegant best of it, and Clive Streeter is a nonpareil among photographers. Congratulations to Marnie Searchwell for her inspired art direction and to Patrick Knowles for his contribution to the book. Finally, Colin Ziegler is always a pleasure to work

For Dorothee

First published in the United States, Great Britain, Canada,
Australia, and New Zealand in 1994 by North-South Books,
an imprint of Nord-Süd Verlag AG, Gossau Zürich, Switzerland.

Copyright © 1993 by Nord-Süd Verlag AG, Gossau Zürich, Switzerland
First published in Switzerland under the title *Der echte Nikolaus bin ich!*
English translation copyright © 1994 by North-South Books Inc.

Distributed in the United States by North-South Books Inc., New York.

Library of Congress Cataloging-in-Publication Data is available.
A CIP catalogue record for this book is available from The British Library.
ISBN 1-55858-318-1 (trade binding)
ISBN 1-55858-319-X (library binding)

1 3 5 7 9 10 8 6 4 2

Printed in Belgium

I'm the Real Santa Claus!

By Ingrid Ostheeren

Illustrated by

Christa Unzner

Translated by
Rosemary Lanning

North-South Books

NEW YORK / LONDON

It was Christmas Eve. Santa Claus's reindeer were harnessed
to his sleigh, and the elves had loaded sackfuls of presents.
Now all that remained for Santa to do was put on his warmest
clothes and check his list to see which children had been good.
Then, with a merry laugh, he flew away.

First Santa Claus came to a big city.

"Oh, goodness," he said to himself. "I think I've arrived much too early! I've never seen the city so crowded."

The streets were bustling with Christmas shoppers, so it was hard for Santa to find a place to set down his sleigh. When at last he did, a stern voice from behind him said, "You can't park here. Didn't you see the sign?"

"But I'm Santa Claus," he protested.

"That's what they all say," said the policeman, but then he stopped writing out the parking ticket. "Listen," he said, "I know what it's like. I was Santa Claus myself once, at the children's hospital. All the same, don't let me catch you again or I'll have to give you a parking ticket."

Santa was confused by what the policeman had said. "Surely there's only one Santa Claus," he thought as he strode down the street, "and that's me."

But everywhere he looked he saw more and more people dressed just like him. One of them, coming the other way, waved at him and shouted, "I see we rented our costumes from the same place! You can tell by the nose. Very lifelike, isn't it!"

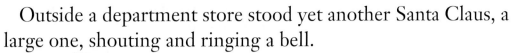
Outside a department store stood yet another Santa Claus, a large one, shouting and ringing a bell.

"Hey, you," he said when he saw the real Santa Claus. "Go and find somewhere else to stand. This is my territory."

Just then a woman marched out of the store, pulling a little girl behind her. Santa Claus had a beautiful doll in his hand, but before he could give it to the little girl, her mother dragged her away.

"Never take presents from strangers!" she snapped.

"Oh please!" cried the little girl. "It is Christmas!"

Santa Claus went into the next building. He knew two boys lived there who hadn't been very good this year. Since he couldn't deliver his presents until everyone was asleep, he decided to speak to them seriously.

Suddenly a tall, thin Santa Claus came rushing down the stairs. "Hello," he said. "Are you looking for Thomas and Martin? I've just delivered some toys to them."

"But those boys haven't been at all good," said Santa Claus.

"It's not my job to tell them that," said the young man. "The toy shop just hires me to make deliveries."

Santa went sadly back to his sleigh. It seemed as if anyone could be Santa Claus now. All a person had to do was wear a costume.

"No one needs me," he thought. "I might as well go home."

Suddenly, three Santas came running out of a bank on the opposite side of the road. One threw a shopping bag straight at him. "Meet us in the forest at midnight!" he shouted as he ran away.

As Santa Claus looked in the bag, police cars came roaring round the corner, their sirens wailing. The bag was stuffed full of money. Those Santas had just robbed a bank! Shaking his head, Santa Claus tossed the bag on his sleigh.

Two policemen ran up. "Stop! Don't move!" shouted one of them. "You're under arrest."

"No, let him go," said the other. "I've seen him before. He's…" The policeman lowered his voice to a whisper, but Santa Claus could still hear what he said: "…the old fellow's not quite right in the head. He thinks he's the *real* Santa Claus." Then he shouted to Santa, "The big red nose, that's real, eh?"

"Of course," said Santa Claus indignantly. He was very proud of his nose.

"See what I mean," the policeman whispered. "He's not one of the robbers. Let's go."

Santa Claus was cold, tired, and miserable.

As he stood in the snow, he saw a woman outside her house, calling her cat. "Hello, Santa Claus!" she said cheerfully.

"You know I'm the *real* Santa Claus, don't you?" he asked.

"Of course," she said, "and I've always wanted to meet you. Why don't you come inside and warm up?"

"The grown-ups don't seem to know who I am," said Santa Claus sadly as the woman poured him a cup of tea.

"That's because they've stopped believing in you," she said. "But the children still love you."

"And do they still like presents?" said Santa Claus.

"Of course," said the woman. "Children love to get presents."

Santa Claus looked out of the window. "It's getting very dark," he said. "I think I'd best be on my way. I musn't let the children down."

Santa Claus thanked the woman for her kindness. Then, just as he was about to drive away, he remembered the bag of money.

"What happens to stolen money?" he asked. The woman looked at him in horror.

"I just heard about a bank robbery on the radio," she said. "That wasn't you, was it?"

Santa Claus told her how the robbers had thrown the money at him. He gave her the bag, and she promised to take it to the police.

"There will be a reward for that," she said.

"Please use it to buy a present for yourself and the cat," said Santa Claus.

All night long Santa hurried from house to house. He piled
the big presents under the Christmas trees and stuffed the
small ones in the stockings hung from mantelpieces.

Just as he was getting ready to go back home, he saw a little
girl waving to him from a window. She was clutching the
teddy bear he had left for her.

"I've stayed up all night to see you," she called. "My brother
says there is no Santa Claus, but I just *knew* you were real!"